THE ANGRY GODS

First published in the UK in 2003 by
Dewi Lewis Publishing
8 Broomfield Road
Heaton Moor
Stockport SK4 4ND
+44 (0)161 442 9450

www.dewilewispublishing.com

A section of *The Angry Gods* first appeared
in *The Jewish Quarterly*, Summer 2000

ISBN: 1899235949

Design & artwork production: Dewi Lewis Publishing
Printed and bound in Great Britain by
Biddles Ltd, Guildford and King's Lynn

9   8   7   6   5   4   3   2   1

THE ANGRY GODS

Wendy Brandmark

DEWI LEWIS
PUBLISHING

To my father and mother

1

Helen, 1972

My mother is a moody woman. Sometimes I find her in the morning with her elbows on the kitchen window sill staring down at the street. She doesn't turn when she hears my step.

'What's wrong?' I ask.

'Nothing. Can't I just look?' She twists round, sees me in my pajamas.

'Aren't you ready yet?' She says, then stares back out the window.

What does she find down there that is more interesting than the life of our house?

'What are you looking at?'

She does not answer but I wait.

'Nothing. I'm looking at nothing.'

I just recently became a woman. When I showed her the brown stains, she cried, then let me lay all Saturday in the living-room with the curtains drawn.

I told her not to tell my father but I knew she had. He had a funny smile that evening like he was ashamed of himself. And he seemed to back off when I came near him. He let me control the television. It was the only time I could remember when he did not sit slumped in the easy chair, his long arms reaching out to turn the channels.

Sometimes I think he looks like an ape. It's the way he stands when he's angry at me, shoulders hunched, his arms dangling by his side, his face thrust forward. My mother says he looks like Jimmy Stewart, why she married him. I think Jimmy Stewart didn't have such a grizzled face in the morning; Nixon's five o'clock shadow has nothing on my father.

I think now he'll let me wear make-up. Last week he grabbed me as I was sashaying down the hall one morning, and wiped away my black eye liner and brown shadow. A half hour's work gone with one smear of his spatula fingers. He said 'What you want to look like that for?'

My mother doesn't care what I put on my face. She paints her lips a bright red, plucks off most of her eyebrows, draws an arc above each eye in brown pencil so she has a permanent look of surprise. But that's only around her make-believe eyebrows; the rest of her face is always telling me something different.

She didn't used to do that to herself. When I was little Marsha my babysitter used to call out to me, 'Come look at your Mommy!' Like she was some movie star. She'd turn from the diamond shaped mirror in the hallway and look beyond us pridefully. Then my father would march into the room and she would suddenly notice us and give Marsha instructions for the evening. Lamb chops in the broiler, frozen beans, my bedtime.

But she's fat now. Her shiny hair is striped with grey, and cut so short that no one knows about her curls. Once when we were arguing in Macy's about my winter jacket, I told her she looked like a prize fighter. She did too, with her flesh bulging out of the short sleeves of her blouse, her belligerent face. She hit me, the first time ever. Right in the middle of the store, she slapped my cheek and the sound jolted all the salesladies murmuring like bees around us.

'I've had enough of your cracks.'

I ran away from her through the store but when I reached the exit I noticed the tag on my sleeve. I was still wearing the jacket I had tried on and hated; I had left my own coat on my mother's arm and had to go back.

Her large face looked suddenly flabby as if she'd been puffed up and then deflated. She gave me a look as if to say 'now you know me so well how do you feel?' She extended her arm and I pulled off the coat and my bag. Then she said, 'Aren't you a fool?'

Someday I won't have to shop with her, won't have to hear her say to the salesgirl after I've slipped on an oversize coat, 'We can take it in and then let it out.' As if I'm going to balloon like her.

2

Sonia, 1955

The Complaint

Not that I scorn mortal man, only
how to explain? That his is a spasm
a moment before he turns his mouth,
the flesh become word,
to shape considerations.

The pain is so deep, like a rat gnawing at my bones, in my spine, my head, yes even in my teeth. 'My little maladies,' the doctor says, but sometimes I am certain he lies that I will never be well again. All weekend I live in the blackness of my room listening to my parents' slippers in the hall.

'Where's Sonia?'

'In bed. Where do you think?'

'Not again.'

Then a whispered conference.

'Sonia.' Someone stands in the doorway. I have been rubbing my eyes and cannot make out who it is.

'Why don't you come? Have a glass of tea with us.' Leo, my eldest brother, a big fleshy man.

'I don't feel well.'

'Don't be so anti-social.' He has a laugh in his voice, but I know he has been sent to pull me out.

'Leave me alone.'

'Sonia, come on. I never get to see you.'

Another figure appears in the doorway.

'What are you begging her for? If she wants to sulk, leave her.' His wife Leah told me it is all my head, all the pain I imagine.

Lying there in the darkness I do not feel so afraid of Leah. I can see her in the hall light, but Leah has to peer into the room to find me.

The two figures leave the doorway and I hear them back in the livingroom. If I go out there now, after they have left me, the baby throwing tantrums, Leah will win.

'A husband would settle her,' My mother says.

'But she's too fussy.'

I am the last to leave. My brothers married from home and I the youngest, conceived when my mother felt her arms grow empty, was expected to follow. But I sit in the evenings watching my father watch television, my back braced by a pillow. I am thirty-one and have not even had a broken engagement. This my mother will not forgive. Do you have a heart, she asks, do you? What's inside there? She jabs my chest with the blunt end of her knitting needle. Every piece of nothing gets married she says after we meet one of my schoolfriends with a husband coiled around her.

I still keep a black and white school notebook but in place of the problems I used to copy from the board I write little poems, lines I wake up with in my mouth and must spit out: 'What has happened to me? Why have I been washed up on this barren shore?'

'Poor Sonia,' I hear Leo say to his children. And if his daughters show signs, if they grow silent at the dinner table or dress in dark colors, they are warned that they can become like me.

In college I was fixed up with men; for one night I endured their chatter about overheads and collateral, their hands on my back as we stood up at the end of a movie. Always there was another couple with us, an established pair who treated us like their children.

Leo once said to me: 'You don't have to love him.' After fifteen years of marriage he and Leah were companions, that's what lasted.

'The rest.' He waved his hands in the air as if to dispel a bad odor.

They have grown alike, Leah a gaunt version of her husband, both with thick glasses magnifying the judgment in their eyes. Leo changed since his marriage; even his affection is calculated; he measures what he can give and retain, what profit can be made,

8

like the businessman he has become. But he is not a success so Leah has had to go back to teaching.

'Bye Sonia,' Leo shouts out.

I try to shout back but my throat is dry and all that comes out is a hoarse whisper. Have I lost my voice as well as everything else?

I reach for the notebook and then lay back with it on my breasts and let the room possess me. Again I creep into the warm brown sea; the water my bed, I float out beyond the edge of the known world. Sea birds call and gulls come down to pick at my clothes till I am naked beneath the blanket of foam.

'Sonia. Are you having dinner or what?' When I was a child she used to entice me to the table by bringing a plate of brisket and potatoes for me to look at and smell but now she lets my food grow cold.

I climb out of bed and stagger towards the doorway. Down the hall I see the table in the foyer where my father and mother wait. So far the tableau in lamplight, like a miniature painting I can never enter.

They watch me approach.

'Finally,' my mother says.

❋ ❋ ❋

I think of it as a heavy red-faced man, arms embracing the cement playground where children line up by class after lunch. In the far corner separated by high gates from the rest of the yard is a small garden, plots of earth dug from cement, where the retarded children grow flowers. The school was built after the war but the Virginia creeper which covers most of the brick walls and even some windows makes the building look much older.

In the autumn the children fill their pockets with the shiny red leaves, let them fall on the floor of the closet as they put on their coats. The leaves grow dry and brown during the winter months and in the spring when I search the closet for the Easter egg paints I hear the crackle of autumn under my feet.

I stayed home on the Monday and Tuesday and now the children are haggard with freedom. The substitute let them draw all day and when they were bored told them stories about her hamster.

During the Pledge of Allegiance, I catch Lewis with his hand on his belly and see Linda throwing bits of white paper on Christine's head. I make them do it again after the loudspeaker shuts down and all the other teachers in the school have begun to call the roll. I never scream like the others to gain control. I stare at a boy till he is ashamed or make him repeat what he has mocked again and again till he sees its value.

The bullying of Christine has begun again. I see it in their eyes when I call the girl's name. They tasted blood these last two days and now they are insatiable.

I cannot understand why Christine attracts so much violence. She is a quiet fanciful child, very thin with a large pale dreamy face surrounded by a halo of fuzzy brown hair. She is bookish, fond of Hans Christian Anderson and the Purple, Yellow and Red fairy tale books, but she does not do well on spelling and arithmetic tests. She squints at the board when I write out problems in long division and the children laugh to hear her answers. Christine laughs with them, that is her problem, laughs at the numbers which seem less comprehensible than talking wolves and paper ballerinas floating to their death in foreign sewers.

I will drill them this morning, first on geography and then spelling. I will not go around the room; that makes it too easy, those already picked on can let their attention wander. I'll chose names at random, not even alternating boys and girls.

They are better at remembering the capitals than identifying the states and countries from the map. The boys pride themselves on their geography but even they cannot find Arizona or Brazil on the unnamed spaces so distant from the Bronx.

'Christine,' I call out, 'the capital of Massachusetts.' I have given her an easy one, the girl might answer right for once and gain some respect.

But Christine's eyes cloud and there is the beginning of giggles in the room. She shakes her head.

Behind her Paul waves his hand wildly. I have seen him stick a paper on Christine's back and will not give him the satisfaction of answering correctly.

I wait, the girl might come forth with the right city.

'Is it Chicago?'

The boys laugh and Paul cannot contain himself any longer and calls out, 'Boston, Boston. It's so easy.'

'Christine the cretin,' someone shouts and everyone takes up the cry. Christine looks confused, as though she doesn't understand the meaning of the taunt hurled at her many times before.

'That's enough,' I say. I walk around the room to where the words emerged. Arthur Moskowitz, a chubby boy with a shiny foolish face.

'I didn't start it,' he whines as I grab him by the arm and pull him up from the seat. He is big, but his strength is so dissipated in flab that it is like pulling up a carcass.

I keep a chair by the side of my desk where I talk to children at the end of term about their report cards. This is where I put loud mouths, the boys who pull up the girls' skirts. They have to sit at the front with their back to the class. Only I can see their faces, and I let them know that I am watching all the time, even while I write on the board. Arthur squirms in the seat; he cannot see what the class thinks of him, cannot know if the laughter is intended for him.

He is close to Christine for she sits in the front row with the other short children. She shrinks back in her seat and looks up at me with pleading eyes: please, please, don't punish anyone else.

The class sobers up; those who shouted look down at the pock-marked wooden desks to avoid my eyes or try to hide themselves behind the heads of their more innocent counterparts. I keep silent for a few minutes, just enough time to strike terror into their small hearts. Then I ask them to take out their notebooks for a spelling test.

'Spelling,' Linda repeats in an awed voice while the others moan. Their faces grow solemn as they wait for me to call out the words.

A low wail which seems to circle the school and come back

11

louder. The children know by now what to do in an air raid drill. They crawl under their desks, bow their heads and place their hands over the backs of their necks to protect their most precious nerve against the rays of the bomb.

I walk around the room to make sure they are all in position. The bigger children have to work hard to fit themselves under the narrow chairs. The only sounds in the room: the creaking of chairs, the breathing of children waiting for the all clear.

I hear what sounds like a sob from the front of the room, an intake of breath followed by suppressed giggling. I follow the sound past the children too frightened to poke their heads out for they believe in the bomb as they once did in Santa Claus. I tap Christine on the shoulder but her laughter grows till she is choking with mirth.

'Get up,' I say, though this is against the rules during an air raid drill. The girl crawls out from the desk, her face flushed. She begins to hiccup as she laughs and cannot stop, not even after the all clear sounds and the others come out from under their chairs to stare at her.

Her face is grotesque with laughter, her mouth wide, her cheeks creased like a crying baby. When I shake her, she begins to hyperventilate; her gasps send the other children running to the closets at back of the room where they hide behind their coats from her.

'She's all you ever talk about,' Irene says.

'But I don't know what to do with her.'

'Leave her alone. They'll stop picking on her. They'll get as bored as I am.'

'You think it's my fault?'

'Please. I'm changing the subject.'

'I only just started.'

We sit along the wall of the deli, so tiny there is only room for one row of tables along the narrow windowless corridor behind the meat counter and grill where hot dogs turn slowly on greasy metal rollers.

Wednesday is the only day we do not bring our own sandwiches to eat in the teachers' room. We like to break up the week with a treat. Irene always orders corned beef lean and watches the man cut off bits of fat. I never know what I want till I enter the smoky, meaty room, the Star of David on its window clouded with grease and vapor, and then sickened by the smell I order a tuna sandwich.

Irene is a small red-haired woman with a round soft face and a sharp tongue. She teaches the 'one' class in the sixth grade; her pupils, most of whom will skip a year and someday go on to college, cower before her fierce intelligence. Once I walked past her class and heard her say to one of the boys, 'You imbecile.' My brother Leo calls her 'piano legs'. She argued with him about Russia and came away the victor; he had bought the capitalist dream, she warned him, and soon he would be bankrupt.

Sometimes I think we are friends because we are the only spinsters in the school apart from the ancient principal, Miss Bates, and Miss Siegel, a very young woman who sings her kindergarten children to sleep, and was discovered one day to be wearing an engagement ring.

Irene calls the others 'hausfraus', the women in their forties and fifties returning to teach after their own children left them. But there is no one Irene does not criticize; she could find fault with the prophets.

'So where were you?' Irene asks.

'I didn't feel well.'

'What's that suppose to mean?'

'My back again.'

'If it's not one thing it's another. You're a hypochondriac you know.' Then with one finger pointing in my face as if she is reprimanding a child, she declares: 'You're frustrated.'

'I'm frustrated because of the pain. Nobody can do anything. '

'You need a man. It's just that simple.'

'Don't talk so loud.' I look around but the man at the counter is busy slicing meat. 'You sound like my mother.'

'Who's talking about marriage? You need an affair, even for one weekend. You're dying for it.'

We have had this talk before, Irene listing the men she has

known and discarded. 'Old clothes' she calls them.

'If I don't have my family nagging me, I have you.'

'So get out if they bother you.'

'It's not that easy. My father would be so hurt. Who knows, it might bring on another stroke.'

Six months ago, Irene moved out of her mother's house up near Fordham Road to live alone in a walk-up apartment on Ninety-Sixth Street. She can't afford the rent so she keeps pushing me to move in.

'Meanwhile you're sick and you don't even know why.'

'The doctor said it might be early arthritis.'

'I've never heard of such a thing. Do you think maybe you have "the change" as well?'

'Don't be so smart.' What she says when one of her pupils talks back. 'I hurt all over sometimes. You don't know what it's like.'

'Don't you think I have pains? I just don't act like such a baby.'

So easy to cry these days as if my body is riven with streams. I try to push back the tears with my fingers. I am dizzy when I stand up, my eyes blurred, my leg banging into the table as I push past.

'Hey, aren't we splitting this?' Irene waves the check at me.

❋ ❋ ❋

I wake to the smell of green peppers frying and bury my nose in the pillow. Why so early on a Sunday must my mother cook the food which makes me sick? Then I remember it is Father's day: my brothers will come, will try to arrive at different times, for they do not like to share the stage. They will lay their gifts before our father but no longer wait for his blessing. The grandchildren give him handkerchiefs, large white translucent squares, like veils, which they buy in Woolworth's, while the sons bring bottles of schnapps and nylon ties.

My father spreads the handkerchiefs on his knees and says they are of a fine material. But he can only speak through one side of his mouth now, his words dropping so slowly from his slack lips, that the children grow impatient and do not stay by his chair to listen.

14

He sits in the livingroom already dressed and waiting, his hands on his knees, his back straight in the easy chair.

'Happy Father's day.' I kiss him. He can no longer grasp my head with both hands and cover my forehead with kisses, press my body to his with such ferocity that I cry out. The stroke loosened his muscles so that he has to work all day to make a fist. Now I hug him while his arms hang by his sides. We are like the lovers I saw in a newsreel during the war, the young soldier with his empty sleeves standing on the bridge waiting for his girl to embrace him.

He stares at me as I draw away, his eyes burning with the words which take so long to reach his mouth. I wait, watching his lips so that I do not miss what begins in a slurred whisper, and when I do not understand, ends with the loud unconnected words of a crazy man.

'Again,' he whispers and when I put my ear closer to make sure, he begins to reach out his good arm.

'Walk to me,' he is saying for I am nearly two and still on my hands and knees, 'To me.' My mother told me again and again: 'Six months I tried and then he has only to hold out his hands.'

Julius arrives first with his daughter and wife Norma. Little people. A compact man snug in a dark suit with worry lines across his forehead who fights litigation cases for the city, and his slender, narrow-shouldered wife, always on the look-out for insults while her dry bony hands pick threads from her clothes.

'How are you Pop?' Julius stands at a distance still afraid of his father even though the big man can no longer push his sons against the wall and whisper, 'Jellyfish. My sons the jellyfish.' But my father does not try to answer him.

'It's too much of an effort for him,' my mother explains. Grey wool hangs from her needles. She always has to be doing something else, even as Julius speaks to her.

Poor Julius. He has her build not my father's and this has been the problem from the beginning. She is so small that her feet cannot reach the floor when she sits on the sofa, and Julius is only a few inches taller.

'Mark my words, you will grow,' my mother told him even after he reached his twenties and was going to night school.

I'm next to her, with the *New York Times Magazine* close by in case I need an escape. Norma sits down on the kitchen chair we dragged into the livingroom, her legs crossed, her arms folded, one foot tapping out her anger. Little Jennifer stands by her chair. When my father catches her eye, she buries her face in her mother's shoulder, but she cannot keep from looking. He is nodding to her, she should come visit him, she is more welcome than her father who still stands before the old man waiting for him to open up his gifts with his good hand.

'Look, your grandpa wants to speak to you. Why don't you go see him?' I tell her.

'She's shy. Let her be,' Norma says. Jennifer buries her head in her mother's shoulder again.

'Come to me,' My mother says, putting down her needles and holding out her hands.

Jennifer pulls her head from her mother and stares at her grandmother.

'Leave her alone already,' Norma complains and begins fussing with the little girl's sailor collar.

But my mother ignores her. 'Come.' She holds out her hands, 'I'll tell you a secret nobody else knows.'

Jennifer looks between the two women till Norma says 'So go.'

She turns to me. 'What's new? You seeing anyone yet?'

'She's fussy,' My mother says, 'So fussy. Eh Sonia? You push them away.'

I shrug my shoulders, lean back on the sofa with my eyes shut; I will not give them anything to feed on.

'Well you won't meet anyone staying home moping.' Norma waits for answer, then turns to Julius who after watching his father drop his gifts unopened on the floor sits down on the sofa between my mother and me. 'Aren't I right, she should go out more?'

'You should you know,' he says. More and more he agrees with his wife, her bitterness now become his for she shows him how blind he has been all his life to insults from his family, how his parents always preferred his brother Leo.

Julius was my favorite brother. He did not pick on me like Leo or laugh when I grew breasts and began to wear stockings. I am taller than him now and broad shouldered, my father's daughter, but once he took care of me. On my eighth birthday when my father was in hospital with the first of his strokes and my mother could not think about a celebration, he took me out to a fancy restaurant on Broadway with pink drapes in the entrance and a reception crowded with mirrors, even a chandelier. The waiter led us down the white carpeted stairs to a marble table where we ordered hamburgers. It was Sunday afternoon and the tables on either side of us were empty. In the corner an elderly woman in a maroon suit and a purple hat whose veil came halfway down her haughty nose sat before a dish of ice cream. She stared unsmiling at me, a big-boned girl too large for her age.

The hamburger arrived on a paper doily with a heart of lettuce and two enormous slices of beef tomato. I began to lift the tomato with my fork but it was so large and fleshy that it fell off. The waiter had been watching and came forward.

'May I cut your tomato for you?' He spoke loud enough for the woman in the corner to cast her unfriendly eyes in my direction again.

It had never happened before. I could not speak, so ashamed that he should understand I was in difficulties. Julius smiled at both of us.

'She's doing all right,' he told the waiter.

'Mom said you were sick last week.' Julius sits forward on the sofa so that he might be speaking both to his wife and sister. 'What was wrong?'

'Just my back. And I had a cold.'

'You're always getting something,' Norma says. Once I was the family baby and Norma had to pay homage to me like all the others, but now I am nothing.

'Maybe you should see a specialist about your back,' Julius says.

'I'm all right.'

Afterwards Norma will say to her husband, 'See what I mean, she doesn't want to be helped. She doesn't appreciate you.' But now she is silent, watching her daughter twist her grandmother's knitting needles.

Julius follows his wife's eyes. 'Should she be playing with those?' he asks his mother. 'She could poke herself.'

'I'm teaching her. She'll be knitting you a sweater already.'

Norma takes this as an affront. Something else she has neglected to show her daughter.

'She's too young to learn.'

'I learned when I was younger than her even,' my mother says, 'You hang over her too much.'

This was what Norma expected, why she holds herself upright in the chair, but before she can speak, the doorbell rings.

'Ah, that's them,' my mother says as if Leo is the guest we have all been waiting for.

Julius looks at his wife and raises his eyebrows slightly so she will be the only one to notice. He does not like to meet his brother and carefully times his visits so that they will not overlap. Five years ago when my father had to retire because of his paralysis, they fought over the sale of his building business, each one trying to bite off a bigger chunk of the substance of their childhood. And then there was the bar mitzvah when Leo rented a whole restaurant on Long Island and said no children under four could come. Julius had to find a babysitter for Jennifer and appear childless at his brother's triumph.

Leo blows into the room on a draught of stale air from the hallway. He bends down to kiss my mother, then walks boldly towards my father and holds out a long box which has been pre-wrapped in silver paper by the liquor store.

'Hello Pop.' When my father does not reach for his gift he places it on his lap and shakes his good hand.

'Your favorite.' He points down to the box.

My father rubs the shiny paper with his fingers and looks up at his son with a small smile.

Leo turns to his brother: 'What you get?'

'I don't know yet.'

'Look. I'm wearing everything.' Leo opens his jacket to show his new shirt already wrinkled across his stomach. 'This too.' He points to his blue and green striped tie. 'My girls.' Then he pushes up his sleeve to show a hairy arm with a large Timex watch. 'Leah.'

'What about Richard?' Julius asks. 'What did he get you?'

Leo raises his eyebrows but says with pride. 'Too busy. What with college and his girlfriend. He always forgets. What do you expect with a boy?'

Leo could make even his son's thoughtlessness into a gift.

'Where's the kids?' My mother looks around Leah as if she expects her grandchildren might be hiding behind their mother's body.

'They couldn't come. They left all their homework to the last minute and Janet had a date.'

Leah pulls up another kitchen chair and sits down. 'What a time we had getting here.'

'Already she's seeing someone? She's so young,' my mother says.

'You forget. Janet just had her sweet sixteen.'

'I'll be dancing at her wedding yet.'

Always the same conversation and then they look at me to see how I am taking it.

But I am watching my father. Jennifer has finally had the courage to go up to him, and she is slowly uncurling his frozen hand, the one which lives a separate life from his body. She pulls it open knuckle by knuckle, stretching the fingers while he watches. There in the flat of his workman's palm, in the hand which built a wooden house for his parents in Riga before he ran from the Russian army, lifted steel girders for a skyscraper in Brooklyn, which pounded the kitchen table when his first building began to sink even as they were signing the bills, there in a hand so calloused that he could never be gentle, lies a tiny doll. The look on my father's face as his granddaughter picks the plastic girl from his palm is one of victory.

19

3

Helen

'Touch wood,' my mother says, rapping my head with her knuckle. She doesn't believe but she's always talking about 'the angry gods', appeasing them like ravenous dogs with pieces of our life, my life. But they are never satisfied.

When I tell her she's superstitious she says, 'Don't give me that.'

But I see her looking up whenever I come home with a good report card. She can hear them already, striking their shields, howling and stamping their feet as they descend on us.

They are quiet these days. And there's nobody around when I come home from school. When I started junior high, I lost my friends; we were all put in different classes. Sometimes I see them in the lunchroom sitting at the long tables with their new homeroom friends, or cross-legged on the floor eating their sandwiches, for there are too many of us in the new school.

My mother says we're all just ants in the universe, trillions of little nothings scurrying around. I'm sick just thinking about it: the ants swarming over their victim, crawling with their crumbs to the nest where they sleep in a brown pile which never ceases to move.

There was a riot the other day in the lunchroom. Everyone started running to see a fight, until Mr Gilman, the dean, yelled at them to go back. When they turned around they crashed into the kids who hadn't heard and were still running. Kids sprawled all over the floor, and some of them started fighting.

I was taking the sex test when it happened. Even though I lied I still scored 'Virgin Mary'. Like any test, it got harder as you went along. 'Ever make out in your pajamas?' All the girls who went to camp got points for that one. 'Ever let a boy take off your blouse? Ever get stoned? Ever perform sixty-nine?' Everyone wanted a medium score: 'Experience shows' or 'Spicy but nice'. Not Sheila

Rosen. She let the whole lunchroom know she was 'Flying in hell'. But when she picked me out of the homeroom to sit next to at lunch, I was glad because before that I had no one.

You have to watch out you don't get mixed up with the nerds which is so easy. Debby Abrams used to lead the others in picking on Clare, our homeroom creep, a tall girl with black eyebrows growing across the bridge of her nose, and a smell of Lysol. Suddenly Debby was the one attacked. They called her 'Abrams the A bra', and now she has to be friends with Clare, otherwise she's alone. She told me once that Clare lives with her mother and sister in a dark one room basement, why she can't see to tweeze those eyebrows.

Sheila passes me a bag of potato chips, her cheeks and lips shiny from eating. If you didn't know about her you'd think she was just a sweet little kid with her pudgy cheeks, freckles and wide blue eyes. It's a shock when she opens her mouth. 'You're a fugitive from a leaking scumbag,' she told a boy who called her a tramp. 'Scumbag' is her favorite word, but I'm still not sure what it means.

This morning she says to me, 'What hit you?' Because I look good for once. I worked on my flip for an hour, wetting and combing and drying and spraying until it was the same all around, a shiny moat of hair I held my head rigid to contain. My eyes are bordered by black lines extended like Cleopatra, and I've given myself a white mouth.

My father told me I looked like a clown but he did not touch my face. He keeps away from me now like I have something wrong with me. 'You can't catch what I have,' I want to tell him. If he knew what I do in the afternoons after school when my mother is out shopping, how I lay in the bedroom with the curtains drawn, shut my eyes and pretend to be with someone else. Usually the boy who works in the grocery across the street, but sometimes it's Sheila. I keep trying to push her face out of my mind but it's like the dream I had. Someone telling me to count sheep, but as they're leaping over the fence they turn into my father and mother.

Sheila tells me a scumbag is what dirty people use. We're walking on Fordham Road, up the hill, then down, while she

21

complains that her boyfriends are always grabbing more and more of her.

'They're pulling, I'm pushing. You get sick of it. You know what I mean?'

I don't, but I mumble something about boys being disgusting. I remember the time a boy on the subway shouted at me, 'Bet you got a big pussy.' It was only later, maybe a year later that I understood what he meant.

We see an old movie, *A House is Not a Home*. Shelley Winters goes out with her boss and he tears her clothes off in the car. She can't go home, she can't go back to work, so she starts up a whorehouse. Then she falls in love but the guy can't get over the fact that she's a madam.

I hear Sheila sniffing next to me. She's still at it when we leave the movie. She's a messy crier, her nose dribbling, eye makeup all over her cheeks. She gets angry when I ask if she wants to go for a soda in Crumb's.

'What are you looking at me like that for?' she says.

'I'm not looking at you any way. I just asked.'

'You think it's so funny?'

'What's the matter with you? Why are you getting like that for?'

'Your mother shoulda used a scumbag.'

I know this is an insult but I don't understand.

'What are you talking about?'

'Don't you know? Don't you know everyone does it?'

'Stop yelling at me.'

'Who's yelling? I'm just telling you your father fucked your mother.'

'Why don't you shut up,' I cried.

'They fucked to get you scumbag.'

My mother slept next to my father; this was how it happened. They turned their faces towards each other and I grew from their mouths like the breath you see in winter.

4

Sonia

'What are you waiting for?' Irene's voice tugs at me.

'I don't know. It's just.'

'Your family's driving you crazy. You ache from them all over your body.'

I turn to watch my children. In the dim cavernous hall where classes line up to march into the assembly and first graders play 'duck, duck, goose', the mothers set up tables for the annual cake sale.

In the morning the children brought down their offerings: tiny sunken cupcakes iced pink and white, the proud issues of mothers; large puffy blueberry muffins bought from bakeries and then repacked in aluminum foil to make them look homemade; the cakes left in their supermarket wrappings, too familiar to be disguised: Devil Dogs, Twinkies, pairs of igloo shaped cupcakes covered in spongy pink marshmallow.

In the afternoon we let the children loose to buy what they cannot get at home. There is an unspoken rule: you never eat what you brought. Like the prince and the pauper, you exchange mothers on cake sale day. While your friends tear at the wrappings of forbidden cakes sent by women who let their own children eat from the hands of strangers, you enjoy the flowery sweetness of a kitchen mother, clean and shining, though her hands are never free of butter and sugar.

Christine's mother had worked hard; there were swirls of vanilla icing on each cupcake and a glazed cherry. The other children stared at the cakes on Christine's desk, but they are careful not to buy them.

'I don't understand you.' Irene stands with her back to the tables where the younger children crowd behind the sixth graders, their small hands reaching wildly beyond the bodies of their older brethren.

'Don't touch, point,' One of the mothers behind the tables shouts, while another stands up and pushes a horde of children back.

'Maybe we better help,' I say.

'Let them cope with it for once.'

This is a day when children's fingers soil the pages of their readers, their chairs, their teachers' skirts, yet Irene wears her good blue suit. It makes her look even smaller, squarer, the straight skirt reaching far below her knees to cover what it can of her short stocky legs.

'Are you going anywhere?' I ask.

'Why?'

'You look dressed up.'

'You mean this drab thing? I wear it for the mothers. It's the same one I wear on open school week.'

'Why bother?'

'So they'll leave me alone. I look like a policeman, don't you think?'

She looks delicate despite her policeman body; her soft face with the red bloom of her mouth drooping, her hair thin and frizzy like a rusty halo.

'No, you look nice.'

'Come on. Tell the truth. This makes me look like I got football shoulders. Feel the padding.'

I put my hand on her shoulder.

'Watch it. They'll think we're lessies.'

Christine passes slowly, her eyes half shut, her mouth smeared with chocolate crumbs and cream. She holds a devil dog in one flat hand.

Irene stares at her. 'I don't care what you say. She's creepy. Like a Martian.'

'Shush. She'll hear you.' Then I call out: 'Christine watch where you're going.'

Christine opens her eyes wide, then seems to shrink from Irene's stare.

'She's not all there,' Irene says.

'I tell you she can hear you.'

Christine continues to stand there watching us. What is it with her? But then I realize she is waiting to be released from us; just by talking to her I made her captive, it was that easy. I want to wipe the girl's mouth. But it would look ridiculous, a girl her age cleaned like a baby.

Irene loses interest in Christine and is back nagging at me to move into her apartment. 'Why don't you come back and look at the place at least.'

'Maybe.' I can't stop watching the girl. She stands in the shadow of one of the pillars. Suddenly she comes forward, holds out her remaining devil dog.

'I don't believe it,' Irene says, 'Is she retarded or what?'

'No Christine. No thank you. Why don't you go buy something for your mother?'

The girl laughs at the idea, would have clapped if not for the cake in her hand. Her face is so white and large on her rag doll body that she seems to float, a full smiling moon through the shadows towards the busy tables under the high latticed windows.

'So you'll come back with me this afternoon.'

'Yes, okay.' I keep an eye on Christine who has reached the crowd of children and stands waiting for an opening.

'You're not even listening. You don't even know what I just said. Hey.'

She pinches me.

'I heard already.'

'So?'

'I told you I'd like to see your place.'

'Don't do me any favors.'

I turn to face her. 'I'm telling you I'd really like to see it. I just don't want to commit myself to anything.'

'You'd think I'm asking you to marry you. Just come and have a look. And then we'll go out for a bite. I got a deli around the corner.'

'I can't. My mother expects me for dinner. My brother's coming over.'

25

'You know for a big girl you're quite a baby.'

The building looks flimsy, a narrow five story walk-up with fire escapes zigzagging down the front. Inside the walls curve, the wooden stairway shakes as we climb to Irene's flat. I think of the apartment I share with my parents deep in a heavy brown double-breasted building.

The door opens right onto the kitchen which leads on either side to the two other rooms. There is no introduction, no hallway or foyer. Anyone standing there can see the whole life of the place.

The livingroom is large, L shaped and contains most of Irene's furniture: a hard brown and beige tweed sofa, a blond coffee table, two easy chairs with wooden arms, a desk, a television, and on either side of the window, which is covered with green venetian blinds, large pale bureaus. All have the cold, clean, square lines of Danish modern. Only the fuzzy rug, the throw pillows provide some sense of ease. Irene looks small as she walks around the room describing how she got each piece, stepping carefully around the angular forms.

'If you come, I'll use this as my bedroom.'

'But you'd have no privacy. There's no door.'

'I could put up a curtain.'

'It wouldn't be fair to you.'

'Wait till you see the size of the other room.'

A box. An oblong box without windows, with just enough room for a single bed, a night table, a chest of drawers.

'I'll have the space and light. You'll have the door. That's what you want, isn't it?'

At home I have the large back bedroom where my brothers used to sleep, where all the heavy old-fashioned furniture which can not fit anywhere else is kept: my oak dresser with the oval mirror, the high boy which I fear will crush me as I sleep, my double bed of golden wood, the walk-in closet smelling of old fur.

This room smells of nothing. The silvery blue walls flicker like an old movie under the dying fluorescent light.

I sit down on the bed and look at myself in the long mirror on the closet door. 'Feels like a coffin.'

'Cozy you mean. Listen. It's just a place to sleep. We can use my room as a living room during the day. Then there's the kitchen.'

'Yeah, maybe.'

'The point is.' She stands before me blocking my image in the mirror. 'You'd get away from them.'

I am thinking that I will have to come naked into this blue light, that the room will clothe me with itself. 'It's starting to grow on me,' I say.

But on the subway home I remember myself in the long mirror, large and wild eyed, a giantess lolling on a narrow bed.

I climb the dark streets up to my house, up through the warm fatty smell of the building. Everyone has had their dinner by now, my mother waiting with a plate she has nursed in the oven.

But when I open the door the place is dark. I turn on the light, walk into the kitchen but the oven is cold and empty. I begin opening up cupboard doors not caring about the noise I'm making. Opening and shutting till I hear my mother coming.

'Where were you ?'

'I told you I was going to see Irene.'

'I got worried. What were you doing out so late? Leo came already. I hope he doesn't think you're being unfriendly.'

She sees me looking around. 'You want something? I didn't know.'

'Don't bother. I'll have a sandwich.'

I put my hand on her shoulder but she shakes it off. 'You're a nuisance you know.'

She's in her nightgown already but she begins pulling bowls out of the icebox, a small woman reaching with little hands for meat and potatoes to feed her big girl.

'What's the matter with you?'

She looks up when she hears me sniffing.

'Somebody give you trouble?'

※ ※ ※

'She's leaving. She's going to move in with another teacher. Tell her she's an idiot.' My mother stands in front of my father with her legs apart, her hands working at her grey wool. But he does not speak, doesn't seem to understand. So she turns back to me. 'Do you think it's nice, you should leave your papa like that?'

'I could be married.'

'But you're not.' Her voice is bitter as if my failures have been her own. 'You wanna turn out like those spinsters? You know they get the change early? It's true. Their insides shrink because they've never been used.'

'C'mon ma, you don't believe that.' But I fear my mother's words, like curses on me from above.

'You see them coming home from work. Shrunken little women rushing to their little rooms.'

My father reaches towards me and I give him my hand. Slowly his hand shuts over it, squeezes tighter, so tight that I want to scream. Finally a word comes out: 'Why?'

'Pop, I'm a big girl. I want my own life.'

'We are your life.' His eyes are wet.

'Look at him,' My mother whispers but loud enough so that he can hear. 'You'll give him another stroke.'

He stares into my eyes. His mouth begins to move and we grow silent waiting. 'So let her go.'

※ ※ ※

'What you want to live here for?' Leo says, 'I can't see it.' He sits back in the easy chair in Irene's room and lets his arms drop.

'You got roaches,' Leah calls out from the kitchen.

'So what else is new?' I say.

'I couldn't live here.' Leo shakes his head. 'You left a nice place. You hurt Pop. And for what?'

'Stop nagging.'

'Who's nagging? I'm just being truthful.'

'Who needs your truth?'

Leah comes back in the room but does not sit down. Leo looks up at her and then says, 'We gotta run.'

'Why not stay for dinner?' I do not want them to stay. There is nothing much in the house to cook, but I want to show them that I have a real life here with meals at correct times.

'We'd love to. But we gotta get home. The kids expect us,' Leo says.

'I thought you said they were always out on dates.'

'Not tonight. Tonight we're a family.'

Irene travels home with me most days, but when I am alone, I sometimes forget to take the train downtown instead of up and have to cross the platform at Pelham Parkway. It feels funny coming home to an empty apartment, free of the smells of my mother's cooking, the roast chicken on Fridays, the blur of candles as I open the door.

Irene cooks canned spaghetti and frozen hamburger patties. She goes out most nights to meetings or classes at the New School.

'It's just a place to hang my head,' she likes to say.

'You mean your hat.'

'No I mean my head, my teacher head. I hang it up and go out a person.'

She has a boyfriend for the weekends, a trim, shiny-faced salesman named Harvey Golden who takes her to movies, dinners at Stouffer's and spends Saturday night and a long Sunday morning in her room. He is the only one of her friends who has not been to college and he admires her for all the things the others cannot see; her generosity in bed, the sadness of her face when she wakes. When he flirts with me I become formal till Irene makes me understand this is his hobby and she does not mind.

She never told me about him, how her room, our livingroom would be closed off for half of each weekend, how I would hear them for they forget that it is a curtain not a door which separates us. It's not the sounds I mind but the conversations:

'Could you with her?'

'She's too big for me. Like mounting an ox.'

'But a beautiful ox.'

I begin to shut myself in my bedroom on the weekends; propped up in the narrow bed, I eat lamp chops, read, write poems in my notebook and fall asleep with the mumblings from the other side of the thin wall I share with the next apartment. When the talking

29

goes on into the night, I plug my ears with wet tissues. The couple next door must sleep alongside me for I can hear the creak of their bed as they lay down, silent with each other after so much fighting. One night their conversation was so distinct that even though I rolled to the other side of the bed, I could not help hearing.

'What am I suppose to do?' the woman said, 'Just tell me what am I suppose to do?'

Murmurs in reply, a sing-song male voice, then the loud flat words of the woman. 'Live on memories?'

Again the murmurs and the return of the woman's voice so close.

'What am I suppose to do? Sit in the house day after day?'

Perhaps the man pulled her back from the wall because their words grew dim. Then she was back again as if she knew she had a listener.

'What am I suppose to do? Just because you're a useless impotent nothing?'

I left my room and shut the door behind me. Irene's light was still on behind the purple curtains and I could hear voices from the television as I stood in the dark kitchen.

The first time I saw the couple from the other side of the wall I was shocked by the size of the woman. She was so fat that she swayed from side to side when she walked and had to cling to the banister as she came down the stairs. Her face was small, her eyes wary behind the black outlines of her glasses. Her husband, with the crew cut and square jaw of an army man, waited for her at the bottom with a bashful smile as if she were descending the staircase in her parents' house for the first time and he was her unworthy date.

'Have you got everything?' the woman shouted and he looked confused as if he had never considered that he might not.

Irene says he is like her child, that's what it is all about. 'They love to fight.'

Once when I went across to borrow a cup of sugar from them, the door was ajar. He was down on his knees barking. The woman came to the door holding her bathrobe closed, but I could smell even before I saw the white stream traveling down her leg.

30

5

Helen

I noticed him before but he was always hidden behind the deli counter. My mother says get the cake mix at Safeway's but I go to the little grocery across the street. She calls it a 'Ma and Pa shop' which means she thinks it's dirty. He's down on his knees, stacking cans of plum tomatoes on the bottom shelves. She wants one of the Betty Crocker marble mixes, chocolate waves through white cake. I can't see it, so I go over and ask him. He follows me down the aisle and stares for a long time at the boxes, then moves them around to see if the marble mix is lurking somewhere behind the others.

'Marble,' he keeps saying, shaking his head, 'I never heard of it.'

My mother would call him a greaser with his pointed boots, tight jeans and shirt with half the buttons open, his curly black hair with each ringlet looking like it's been oiled. He's so dark, I thought at first he was black, but now I figure he's Puerto Rican. I was hoping he'd be a Carlos or Mario, but I hear the man at the cash register call out 'Billy'.

'Just a minute. I'm coming.' He turns to me with a bashful face. 'You know I don't see it.'

'That's all right. You're probably out of stock,' I say and let him go to the front where some woman wants to know the price of a can of chunky chicken soup.

I wait, hoping he'll come back to me, but he's down on his knees again stacking those plum tomatoes. He looks up and notices me still standing at the far end of his aisle and comes over.

His smile is something I hadn't counted on. 'Still no luck?' He stands with his hands on his narrow hips. 'Why don't you buy a different one?'

Just in time I stop myself saying 'that's what my mother told me to get'.

What I like about him is how seriously he takes it all. He pulls a yellow cake mix from the shelf. 'This is what my sister makes.'

It's not even Betty Crocker.

When I hesitate, he says, 'My sister makes the most beautiful cakes with this, I'm sure of it.' He looks me straight in the eyes and then winks.

My mother says, 'What you get this for? I told you the marble. What are you, blind?' Then she looks at the box closely. 'What's this anyway? Some kind of junk.'

I decide that if she asks me to return it I won't go. I'll tell her the manager tried to feel me up. Because what will I say to him? That my mother told me to, something creepy like that? And then to have to see his disappointed face when I say that the mix his sister made so well was no good.

'They didn't have the marble. Somebody said this was good so I thought.'

She's looking at the directions on the package. 'What kind of mix is this? You have to add half the ingredients. They must have seen you coming.'

'I did my best.' I've got some tears in my eyes but she doesn't notice.

'Just do me a favor. The next time I ask you to get something don't be so creative.'

It wouldn't have been cool to go back the next day so I wait till the end of the week. When I walk in I take off my coat so he can see me without the heavy armor my mother forces me to wear. He's kneeling on the floor, washing out the dairy case. I can see sweat stains on his jersey shirt, damp hairs at the back of his neck.

As I walk towards him, I catch sight of myself in the round mirror like a shield they put up to catch shoplifters, my face with a silly welcoming smile growing smaller and smaller while my hips broaden. Just like my mother. I know before I even speak to him that I've been a fool to come in.

He doesn't see me at first, he's so busy scrubbing. So I walk past him around the store, picking up a bag of taco chips and a coke and come back along the dairy case where he's filling up a shelf with containers of skimmed milk.

I pretend to be looking at the margarines. When he happens to turn in my direction, I say, 'Hi'.

He smiles so I go on talking.

'The cake mix was good.'

He looks confused so I say, 'The mix you told me to buy, the one your sister makes, it worked out great.'

'Oh yeah.'

'I made it yesterday and everyone was saying how good it was.'

My mother had pushed the box to the back of the cabinet where the cockroaches would feed on it. She made her upside-down cake instead.

'My sister makes beautiful cakes.'

'Yes, I know.'

Again the smile and he's back stacking the milk.

'So long,' I call out. My voice has a thin, high sound like it's coming from somewhere hollow inside of me.

'Bye bye.'

Since I stopped sitting with Sheila at lunch, I've been discovered by a group of the popular girls, the same ones who pick on Debby Abrams and Clare. They were impressed by how I put down Sheila after that time on Fordham Road. She came up to me just as I was waiting on line to get my food.

'Hello stranger,' she poked my back. I made my face sour, so she said, 'What's with you?'

'Nothing. I'm just sitting somewhere else.'

'What are you afraid of?'

I shrugged my shoulders.

'Scumbag,' she said real loud so that everyone on line turned to stare at us.

'Scumbag yourself,' I said in a low voice but she heard me. Maybe it was the first time anyone used her word against her.

She sits with two boys now, not her boyfriends but faggoty little kids with high voices who act like they're protecting her. 'Palace guards' we call them, but her gate is ever open.

At my new table the faces of the popular girls scrunch up as they talk about Shelia. They're all so angular, especially Bonnie Fisher and Michelle O'Brien, that when they lean forward I'm lost in a forest of pointy chins and elbows. Everyday it's the same. 'Will you look at her,' someone says as Shelia passes, her tits flopping around, her boys trailing behind her. 'She just gives it out free. What a slob.' Everyone nods their heads, even me, but they're bored already. 'Who will we have next?' Is the question on everyone's mind. 'Not me, not me.' A look goes around the table. Someone brings up the name of a kid, maybe even a teacher and we all relax for a while.

My mother's impressed that I run with a crowd now. She says, 'why not invite them over'. She even offered to make one of her marble cakes. But she doesn't understand; they would devour me, our dinky little apartment, my father's bowling trophies, my fat mother, as they sat together on the bus back to Riverdale. The marble cake would not be enough for them.

'You're unsociable,' she says when I refuse her offer.

She can talk. My father has to practically drag her to bagel brunches and parties with 'the crowd', how he describes his bowling buddies. She's always saying 'they're his friends.'

I miss Sheila but there's no way I can reach her now for the queen has warned the palace guards against me. They laugh as I pass for she imitates my nearsighted look. She will not let me back in where the others enter so freely.

6

Sonia

Nightfall, The Museum I

The tomb of some clay gone queen
must hold me
till the guards fasten the doors against still
creatures, stones cut with the unfathomable.
I emerge
skin cool glass, nipples like pebbles
my legs have lost their feeling.

I have begun to go out alone in the evening after Irene leaves for one of her classes. It is always a spur of the moment decision, that's the way I like it. And if I have already put on my nightgown, I do not change but cover myself with my bulky grey coat, buttoning up before I close the door behind me.

At first I explore the streets around the apartment. Because I imagine myself invisible, I feel safe in the darkness; when I approach a stranger under a streetlight, I draw up my collar, as if my coat has become part of the concealing sky. This was what I always wanted to do up in the Bronx, but I could never stray from the streets around our house. My mother would say, 'Where are you going so late?' I knew they would be waiting for me in the living room and the waiting was tugging at my back.

I walk quickly for dawdling will make me stand out on the street. Our neighborhood is dead at night; the dentists' and doctors' offices, the drugstores and coffeeshops only stay open during the working day. Nobody stands in the doorways of candystores talking here, nobody hangs around. Sometimes I see a lamp high up in one of the brownstones where some doctor is working late, before I am plunged again into the dark barren labyrinth.

One night I walk uptown, avoiding the wide avenues where the flash of carlights intrude, giving my body back its substance. Suddenly I come upon a street where Negro children edge forward in a game of giant step, sounds of dishwashing come through the bright windows and men smoke and talk on stoops. Nobody seems to notice me but I feel exposed as if the night has left me, has taken human shapes; and I become visible, a large white woman in coat concealing her nightgown. Up in the Bronx the Negro streets lay far south of my parents' apartment, near subway stations which flash by in the tunnel like names in Hades.

I know I should get away but continue to walk north past a schoolyard where teenage boys play basketball, past the dim lights of small groceries and candy stores where girls in white organdy dresses hover over the counter, till I reach a broad main street brimming with carlights, the sidewalk a carnival of stalls, shoppers and speakers hectoring small groups of men. A Negro man thrusts a newspaper at me and when I refuse to take it, walks behind me whispering 'white devil woman', tugging at the belt of my coat like a hungry child.

I lose him in the subway. I catch an express train and as we pass the stations I walked through I think of a long corridor of open doors like the hallway of my school. I have only to shut the door on those streets to forget them. I am safe again in the warm funnel.

But my nightwalks are not the same again. The quiet streets irritate me; the solemn brownstones with their polished brass doorknobs, their neat rows of doctors' buttons, the drugstore with its display of Milk of Magnesia in the glow of the nightlight. Yet I cannot stay in, the stillness of the apartment chafes against me, my skin so tender that I roll back and forth in the bed crying.

I return one night to the streets which I cannot believe exist without me, whose light gives me form and substance. Yet I am a ghost weaving through women who call past my body to each other, children who do not pause from their game of catch when I cross the street, a ghost rising above the jubilant voices in church.

I end my walk on the wide avenue, a river where all the little streets feed. Here I am noticed; men strut alongside me asking and then answering their own questions in soft voices. 'Why are you all by yourself? You must be lonely. Why don't you be more friendly? You're shy. A beautiful woman like you. Shy. Must be.'

The man with the newspaper is suddenly by my side. He seems to smile at me. Does he remember? Again he thrusts the paper at my face.

'We're going to make a new Africa. You read about it.'

I shake my head and walk away but he follows.

'What? Are you prejudiced or something?' He grabs my arm but I pull away.

When the boys in school walked behind me calling 'Christ killer', my father told me never to run away: 'You don't want your enemies they should smell your fear.' So I try to quicken my pace without seeming to. He follows behind, now beside me, now running in front of me with a mocking laugh.

'You think you can come here and just leave? You think you can leave just like that?' Now he screams at me as we rush along like a pair of fighting lovers.

He has driven me far from the subway entrance and now I look for refuge on the street: a pawnbroker, a donut shop, a narrow bar with the door open where men laugh as we pass and someone calls out, 'Leave her alone man, she be too big for you.'

In the midst of the crowds I see another ghost, an old man dwarfed by his black top hat and long coat moving slowly in the opposite direction.

I go to him. 'Mister,' I say, 'Can I walk with you?'

The man seems not to hear for he continues walking, passing his cane before him as if he is blind.

My pursuer moves away but I can see him waiting, a small dark wraith. 'That man is bothering me,' I say, 'if you walk with me maybe he'll go away.' But the old man does not turn to me. I hear him mumble some words, press my head closer, and understand that he is praying.

Would he mind if I tuck my arm in his? We could stroll together, each guarding the other. When I put my hand on his arm he recoils; he can neither hear nor see me but he knows my touch is unclean.

My pursuer comes forward: 'Talking to yourself crazy woman.'

I pause before racks of nightgowns, slips and dresses outside a women's clothing store. Will he not be embarrassed to follow me in there, where women fish for underpants from a cardboard box and stand before long mirrors pressing bras against their bodies? But he does. Under the bright lights I face him, a small, square light-skinned Negro in a dark suit whose hands cannot stop moving.

'What do you want from me?'

He stops speaking for a moment to look at me, he is still smiling but the eyes behind the heavy black rimmed glasses are full of hatred.

'Why don't you leave me alone? I've done nothing to you.'

'Leave me alone,' he taunts in a whiny voice, 'Why don't you leave me alone?'

I run from him through the racks of silky nightgowns across the street, leaving him stranded at the lights. I am on my own for a few blocks. 'Maybe this is the end of it,' I mumble. Then I hear footsteps and turn so he cannot leap on me. He is breathing hard but still he nags at me with a litany of questions.

We are beyond the stores now, beyond the crowds, and soon I will be left alone with him on the darkening street. Ahead I see lights and run to a red brick building; through the high bright windows I can see people moving as if in slow motion past bookshelves. I am certain he will not follow me into the library but he rushes past as I push open the heavy glass door.

I walk towards the white woman stamping books and wait for her to finish before leaning over the desk. 'This man is following me. Could you call the police?'

'The police? You call the police on me?' the man cries, more hurt than alarmed.

'Hush,' the woman says, then turning to me, 'you better talk to the librarian.' She points to a desk at the far end of the room where a man sits half-hidden behind a pile of books.

I stand before him with the other, my shadow, now grown quiet beside me. The librarian's broad forehead is creased with the attention he is giving his work. He holds an open book in one hand and with the other writes on a white index card.

'This man is bothering me.'

The librarian looks up at the two of us: 'George.' He sighs. 'George, leave her alone.'

'But she insults me.'

'Go home George. What you want to waste your time with her for?'

George looks ashamed and turns away.

'The man's a fool. He thinks we should all go back to Africa. All our problems solved. We'll farm the Sahara he says.'

'I didn't take his newspaper, that's how it started.'

'It wouldn't have mattered what you did.' The librarian looks me over. 'What are you doing around here?'

'I was just taking a walk.'

'A walk? Come on. Where do you live?'

When I tell him, he asks, 'What are you, slumming?'

'No I tell you I was walking. I get restless at night.'

'Then you better go home now. George won't give you any more trouble.' He goes back to writing on his index card, and I begin to wander around the library.

I think I see George's face outside the window, with his smile like a Halloween mask. I am back before the desk of the librarian. 'Please can you do something.'

'Why don't you go home, I told you.'

'I think I just saw him out there.'

'What do you want me to do, put the cops on him? George is harmless. He's all mouth.'

'I just don't want him following me home.'

'You think he'd do that? You think he could even walk up your front stairs. He doesn't even exist outside these streets.'

He looks down at the open book but I know he is not reading. I do not leave. I am used to waiting till my children come around, it does not bother me to stand silently before this stranger with the weary face.

He is thinking about me as he smoothes the pages down. He raises his head. 'You still here?' I fold my arms across my breasts.

'Okay, okay. If you can wait fifteen minutes, the library will be closing. I'll walk you to the station.'

He is tall with a broad proud chest and the beginnings of a paunch. His hair is not slicked down like most of the Negro men I see, but cropped close and like his beard streaked with grey.

When he takes my arm as we cross the wide street, I want to shake him off, to say as I had done as a child that I can cross myself.

'You think I'm the bogeyman?'

'No.'

'Then relax.'

But having to walk close to him and yet apart unbalances me; I stumble and fall against him.

'Been drinking?' He laughs, puts out his hand to steady me.

My mother always said they smelled different, that you could always know even if you were blindfolded when a colored man was near. But I can only smell myself for I am sweating in the cold night air and a perfume like the odor of a greenhouse rises from my body.

I search for something to say which will not make me appear ridiculous. 'How do you know George?'

'He's always around. After you meet him once, you keep meeting him.'

'He followed me last time I came here. I thought he recognized me.'

'Not you. He doesn't see you. You're just any white devil.'

He gives me a look and I am burning all over.

'So what do you do when you're not slumming?'

'I'm a schoolteacher.'

'A schoolteacher.' He laughs. 'I don't believe it'.

'I am. I teach fourth grade.'

'You don't look the type. I was one once. Years ago.'

'Why did you give it up?'

'It took too much out of me. I wasn't doing anything but that. I was teaching English in Morris High School. The students were like vampires, more blood and more. Besides everything was

40

different then.' He grows silent, chewing over the past.

When we reach the subway entrance he says, 'So you'll be all right now?'

I nod my head but do not move.

'Then why are you sending me those feelers with your eyes? Eh? If you want me to come with you woman, say it.'

'I guess I'll be all right.'

'You guess?' He begins to guide me down the subway stairs but I am stiff in his arms.

'What is it now?'

'I don't know you.'

'Relax. I'm old enough to be your father. Come. We have to get you home in one piece.'

We are silent with each other on the train. He leans back in the seat, rests his hands on his thighs and shuts his eyes, while I sit forward reading the stations to make sure we're going the right way.

After we climb out of the subway on the other side, he takes my hand. He is rubbing my palm when we reach my building. 'You gonna invite me in?' He asks, then laughs before I can answer.

'Come.' He pulls me against him, his hands moving inside my coat as he kisses me.

'What you got on under there?'

'My nightgown.'

Black gashes on the frozen sea. My father waves to me as he drifts away on an ice floe. He is young again as if he has never been my father.

'Papa,' I scream out for the dark waters have driven him to the edge of the world.

'Papa I will die.' But he cannot hear me.

I wake to an animal cry, the woman on the other side pounding the wall in time to her sobs. The murmurs of the man, then her voice: 'What am I going to do? Just what am I going to do if you leave me?'

❆ ❆ ❆

He tells me he has no time for romance, why his wife walked out on him. In the evenings after he comes home from the library, he sits at his desk writing poetry. A tiny press down in the Village published three books of his verse. He is known down there. Caleb Pink. He renamed himself after a singer he heard as a child. Who he was before he will not say.

At first we meet on what he calls 'neutral territory': a movie theater in the Fifties, the Shamrock Bar up on 103rd Street, and at my insistence the museum.

Caleb wants to see the dinosaurs, but I pull him away from the crowded room down a dim hallway to 'Scenes from Nature', bright glass cases bursting in the silent darkness like dreams: the Arctic, the African bush, the Amazon rainforest, the Alpine meadow.

We stand before the seashore: a horseshoe crab making its way across the red dunes, a starfish curled and dead in the sun, a tern searching the barren waters.

'Reminds me of the end of the world,' he says.

'I love it here.'

'Why are you whispering?'

'I don't want to scare them,' I say, 'When I was little I thought they weren't dead, just waiting for someone to switch them on. To me they were more real than the animals in the zoo. Than anyone for that matter.'

'So you were an odd child.'

I want to say how afraid I was in a house of adults picking on each other, how the ringing in my ears ceased when I visited the dumb animals and birds.

'I thought that after everyone left, they came alive.'

'Like dolls in a toystore.'

'I'm serious.' But I know they are always alive, I have only to step inside the case to hear the wings of a hawk.

'So who would make them live again after their insides been taken out?'

'I didn't know that. I thought God would do it.' Not the God of Abraham, not the angry God who poisoned Cain with envy and let Isaac tremble beneath the knife.

42

'It makes my skin crawl this place. Like a morgue,' he says. 'We never came here. My mother was always busy on some church committee. And my father he wouldn't come here. He'd say that's for white folks with time for such foolishness.'

'But it's educational.' I remember passing a Negro family all dressed up for Easter, Julius saying in a solemn voice, 'You see? Even colored people have dreams.'

'Not that he had much time for us. He was a big man in Harlem. A lawyer. Everyone came running to him when something went wrong. Big daddy make it all right again. And he did.'

'Really.'

'Yes really. I lived in his shadow for thirty years. But that's another story.' He turns to me. 'What did you think I'd say? He was a porter? Maybe a sharecropper?'

'No. I'm just impressed.'

'Come on. Admit it. You thought I'd say he was too busy picking other people's crops to tend to his own.'

'You know you speak in metaphors. All the time.'

He takes my face in his hands. 'You know you're beautiful. Anyone ever tell you that?'

I want to say, 'You won't be like everyone else? You won't disappoint me?' I try to move my head but Caleb holds me fast, my face like clay in his large warm hands.

He draws me back into the darkness. 'This is my only chance. You won't come home with me.'

'I will. Just give me time.'

'Making love in a morgue. Should be the title of my next poem.'

'It's not a morgue. I feel more alive here than anywhere else.'

'You can't mean that.'

'Yes I do. I think I do.'

'But I can tell you're a passionate woman.'

I blush but he cannot see.

'The trouble with you is you spend too many nights in that hothouse apartment of yours.'

I leave him in the darkness to walk to the next case. A mother bear with her cub feeding at a stream, a possum hiding beneath a bush, behind them a painted mountain, a full orange moon. You could stand in front for a long time and not see the possum or the owl with its beak in the belly of a mouse. I heard mothers tell their kids how cute the bear was, not scary at all.

He comes up behind me, his hands finding the soft parts of my back.

'I bet you make the pillow tired every night eh?' he whispers. 'Because it's all raging inside you. That's why you think you'd be peaceful in these still lives.'

'I just thought if I could stay inside there.'

'What do I have to do? Break through the glass to get to you?'

And then what would happen? When the bitter air rushed in, the animals shriveling into corpses, me the woman dragged out of paradise in *Lost Horizon*. The bride in the tower on her wedding night who sees not her husband but her own aged face in the mirror.

7

Helen

When I ask my mother what 'promiscuous' means she gives me a funny stare and says, 'it's when you lose control'. I'd seen the word in an old psychology book they keep in the house and figured out the meaning, but I just want her to talk.

'I don't understand.'

But she's already turning away. 'Why don't you look it up in the dictionary?'

My new friends at school don't talk about sex the way Shelia did. They act like it's a dirty joke everyone knows so they don't have to say. Only I don't know. I'm wondering why we all have to do something everyone laughs at. My parents' psychology book gives names to everything I think and do. In the chapter on teenagers they say that if boys take up sports they'll stop masturbating which is a habit 'detrimental to mental health'. About girls they say nothing.

I lucked out in Woolworth; I was just passing through the store to get out of the rain when I spotted the marriage manuals on a carousel with *The Joy of Cooking* and *Portnoy's Complaint*. Just like the new wives they're always talking about I need the details, the diagrams. They're all written by doctors twenty years ago; the covers say 'revised version' but you know they've never changed anything.

At first I felt sick standing there between the candy counter and the cosmetics, the smell of the store like old socks coming up through the perfumes and the jelly beans while I read about 'breaking the hymen'. The diagrams of positions are much worse than the pictures in *The Joy of Sex*, passed from table to table at school but which nobody believes in. Like having an operation every night till a baby comes out. Even the girls on their back in the tampex directions are not so miserable as these women who have to bear the weight of their husbands.

45

But now I can't go a day without a trip to Woolworth's. I keep a book with a picture of a woman fainting in the arms of a pirate in one hand in case someone looks at what I'm reading and sometimes when the store is crowded I slip the marriage manual inside the other. Once I saw one of my mother's friends but she didn't notice me shoving one of the books back on the carousel. She told my mother I was always reading even in Woolworth's.

So I'm safe till a salesgirl appears one day with a carton of books. I walk around the store while she fills up the empty spaces on the carousel. When I return she's gone leaving fresh copies of the manuals for me. But just as I'm starting to read, she comes up behind me.

I've seen her before at the make-up counter, a tall sour girl with a flat body, square glasses on a square face which never smiles. She reminds me of my aunt Leah. She was always telling us not to touch. We used to torment her by keeping our hands in the air over the counter. She'd follow us as we walked, our hands raised as if we were casting spells over the foundation creams, the lip gloss, the shadow, the tearproof mascara. She never got the joke.

'Are you buying?' she asks.

I can't say yes. I try to hide the cover of the manual with my hand for I had forgotten to pick up my camouflage book.

'This isn't a library.' She takes the manual from me without looking at the cover and puts it back on the carousel. 'People have to buy these books. They don't want dirty fingers on them.'

Driven out of Woolworth's, I begin searching through my parents' bedroom. I don't know exactly what I'm looking for, some evidence, some proof that what the manuals say is true. I start with the chestrobe, a big golden brown curvy thing like a bear on his hind legs. Four deep drawers on one side and a little closet on the other where my mother keeps her coats. Each drawer has a different smell: dusty and metallic on top where my father puts his binoculars, his bowling ball, the camera, boxes of curled photographs from the Adirondacks: my mother all in black, her favorite non-color, perched on a rock overlooking a river, waving like a seal. The second drawer smells of cologne and contains my father's shirts, some still with their cardboard. All of them look the same, the safe white or pale blue buttondowns for his store, the checkered short-sleeved ones for when we go to the country. Once he went to work with the piece of cardboard still in the collar. 'It felt good,' he told my mother when she pulled it out, like someone had finally starched his shirts the way he wanted. 'Fairies' he calls the men he sees sauntering down Third Avenue in bellbottoms, turtlenecks and jackets, heavy pendants swinging from their necks.

It isn't till I reached his underwear drawer that I feel like maybe I do have dirty fingers. It has a funny smell, a combination of deodorizer and birdseed. The undershirts are all in one pile, the boxer shorts in the other. I'd seen him at dinner in one of these outfits. I pick up one of the shorts, holding it by the tips of my fingers at first. Then I put my hand in to discover a little net underpant where he keeps himself imprisoned. No wonder he's always so restless, pushing at himself, scratching when he thinks no one's looking. I examine the other shorts but they have no net and I see no trace of what the manual calls his 'ejaculation'. At the bottom of the drawer I feel a rubbery thing and begin blushing for this must be it, the scumbag, the douche. Then I pull out a pink oblong bag like a waterbottle with a long tube at one end and think what a jerk I am. It's the enema my mother used to purge me with.

'Let it go,' she would say, 'Loosen up your behind and let it go.' I'd be lying on their bed with my pants down, the side of my belly making waves, my hole tender from trying too hard. Then I had to go running to the bathroom.

She'd wait outside the door. 'All out?' she'd ask.

'I don't know,' I'd mumble.

She'd tap on the door because she hadn't heard me. 'You all right?'

When I emerged, my legs trembling, she'd whisper, 'All out now?' I would nod my head and she'd hug me and not let go till we had walked down the hall to the livingroom where I would lay in state all day with a plaid flannel blanket over my legs.

What was it that made this more of an achievement than the pictures of snowmen I drew for her or the napkin holders made from two paper plates or my teacher saying I was one of her shining lights? You'd think my shit was stored in her body, that I let it go for her sake, her alone, when all I wanted was for the pain in my belly to go away.

I put the enema bag back under the shorts, making sure that everything was as I had found it. There was one more drawer, the deepest one at the bottom where my mother keeps her sweaters, but I can find nothing in the folds of the cool dark wool. I slide my hands down the back of the drawer and pull out the long blue felt purse I had made for her on Mother's day with 'Sonia' stitched in red wool across the front and the little clasp the teacher put on for us. I must have been in the third or fourth grade and still she keeps it. It is stiff and when I undo the clasp, I find two black and white photographs inside, one of my mother with her arms around a black man and the other of the man alone standing in some park in his winter coat smiling. I look at the backs but my mother hasn't written anything. Usually she dates them and writes some description. I turn the photos over again, so long ago it's almost not my mother. However much I blink and shift the photos from one hand to the other, my mother and the black man remain close.

She told me about boyfriends, the rich one who asked her to marry him after daddy proposed, who pleaded as she mounted the steps to her building so that she felt like a queen rejecting him; the small restless man who became an actor but never had more than bit roles. 'There he is,' she'd say pointing to the television. You have to look quick or you'll miss him. Then there was Arnold with the jellyfish hands who wooed her in Crotona Park when she was in high school. 'He never married,' she'd say solemnly. Always she seemed larger than them as if they dwindled in her presence. But this man who held her stood a head taller and must have been as old as she is now.

I sit down on my parents' bed with the sunlight warming my face. I stare till I'm seeing double, till the black man and my mother rise from the photo and my mind is full of nothing but them. Then I hear the key in the door and my mother shouting at me to take off the chain. I'd put it on so they couldn't sneak up on me.

When I get up the room goes dark, and I have to brace myself against the bed to keep from fainting. All the time she's hollering and ringing the doorbell. I put the pictures back in the purse, shove it down the back of the drawer and run to the door.

'What you do that for?'

'I get afraid when I'm alone here.'

'You know I got bundles in my arms.' She puts two large brown bags down on the table. Out of breath as usual. It's all the weight she's carrying not the bags of food.

Maybe I'm staring at her funny because she tilts back her head as if to ward off my eyes and then goes into our routine.

'Staring at something girlie?' she says.

'No nothing much.'

8

Sonia

Nightfall, The Museum II

He not prominent
not the Pharaoh marching one foot forward in place
or the Greek alabaster stride.
His date vague, maker unknown, cast in obscurity
beyond reach of the moon.
My hands must be eyes.

'When are you going to invite me up?' he asks.

'There's nothing to see.'

'What are you hiding? A husband? You got a husband cooped up there? Or do you think your roommate would holler?'

It isn't that. Irene always professed sympathy for Negroes. But I am keeping him for myself.

We go up one night, when I know she's at a meeting. Caleb balks at my narrow bed. 'I'm not going in there.'

'Who said you could?'

He wanders into Irene's room. 'She pay more rent than you?'

'No.'

'She should. She pushed you into a little cell.'

'You don't understand. She got the flat first and then invited me.'

'You don't have much sense do you? She's got a room twice the size of yours. She should pay more. It stands to reason.'

'But I like my room. I've got the door, don't you see?' I swing it shut.

'I'd go crazy in here in no time.'

'Shush,' I say for he is standing by my bedroom wall and the couple on the other side have begun.

'How long do I have to wait?' the woman asks. Her voice has gained back its scorn.

The man mumbles something in reply but this does not satisfy her. 'I'm saying how long?'

'You have to listen to that? Jese you got the short end of the stick.' Caleb taps on the wall. 'What is this? Cardboard?'

'Don't do that. They can hear.'

There is some commotion on the other side of the wall. 'I don't care,' the woman shouts, 'Why should I care? I'm drying up.'

'Let's get out of here before we have to hear anymore.'

'But where?'

'We'll go slumming. We'll go to my place.'

His living room is with crowded with heavy fancy furniture: flowered easy chairs with curved arms and legs, a stiff high backed sofa with scrolls for arms, an oak bookcase carved with anchors, a golden brown cabinet whose doors open to reveal a television.

'My wife's taste,' he says. 'When we split up I told her to take it all, but no she says she can't fit these monstrosities in her mother's house. So can I sell them? No. Maybe someday I'll want them she says. Someday her favorite word.'

'Your mother?' I pick up one of the photographs on the cabinet.

He nods then points to the other. 'My girl.'

His daughter in her white confirmation dress, braids around her head, thin face, big big solemn eyes. 'She's cute.'

'Cute? She's beautiful.'

I turn away, look up at the framed profiles of strange black men on the wall. When I ask about these, he names them Kenyatta, Nkrumah, Marcus Garvey.

I feel the weight of his hands on my shoulders and move away. I stand before the window, but all I can see is the blind wall of a church. I begin searching through the bookcase for the volumes he says are his. He comes from behind, his arms around me so tight I cannot escape.

'Now,' he whispers, 'because I can't wait any longer. Now. Because I'm not a young man.'

※ ※ ※

We're sitting on the benches during recess, one of the few times our classes are let out together. Irene seems in awe of me. 'What do you think your family will say?'

'They don't have to know.'

'They're bound to find out if you keep seeing him.'

'Since when do you care so much about what my family think?'

'I don't. I'm just saying you'll have to tell them sometime and I think they'll go crazy.

She spoils everything, like the women whose touch curdled milk.

'I must say you have good taste.'

'What's that supposed to mean?'

'Don't get on your high horse. All I'm saying is that he's attractive. And I've heard of him. I think he once did a reading at the Y. How old is he anyway?'

'I don't know. I suppose in his forties.'

'Are you kidding? He's fifty if he's a day. They always look younger.'

'Well I don't care.'

'Why should you?' Irene pauses; she tries to get me to look at her. 'Tell me, are you sleeping with the guy?'

'That's none of your business.'

'Because I've got a doctor who can fit you with a cap.'

'Don't look so dumbfounded. You don't want to get pregnant do you? And with a Negro baby?'

'I thought you were progressive.'

'Just forget it. I'm not telling you anything anymore.' Irene sits up straighter on the bench. 'You're a fool, a naive fool.'

We watch the children break from their groups and then join together again like the colored glass inside a kaleidoscope. Beyond their dancing bodies Christine is splayed out against the metal fence. We're too far away to see her expression but her face is very white against the black of her coat and hat.

The boys are playing the prisoner game; one team catches the girls, makes them stand against the fence until the other team of boys comes along to free them. The popular girls are freed first and stroll slowly through the yard talking. But no one has rescued

Christine. Several times she tries to leave the fence but the boys fly at her, make her stand with her arms raised and pretend to tie a rope around her wrists.

I'm on my feet but Irene has been watching too. 'Leave her alone, why don't you?'

'But look at her.'

'You've got to let her cope herself. She's not always going to have you around to fight her battles. Anyway the other kids will only bully her more if you interfere.'

'I don't know.'

Christine makes another attempt to escape and this time reaches the middle of the yard before a boy catches up with her. She begins shaking her arms, opening and closing her hands in imitation of some Disney stepmother. The boy runs to me.

'Christine's acting creepy. Look at her.'

'Why don't you just leave her alone? She wouldn't act that way if you just let her be.'

'She says she's putting a spell on me. She says I'm going to die. Tell her to stop.'

'Just ignore her.'

Christine drops her arms and begins walking to where two girls have begun turning a jump rope for a round of double dutch. She doesn't join the line of girls waiting to leap into the slapping rope but stands watching with a smile on her face as if her victory is enough for her.

'God, I'm glad she's not in my class,' Irene says.

'You're right,' I say with my eyes still on Christine.

'About what?'

'You said leave her alone. Let her fight her own battles.'

'Oh that. I thought you meant.'

'If you want to know, he takes care of me.'

❄ ❄ ❄

'Don't get too comfortable in there,' Caleb says before he leaves me in his tiny kitchen with the lamb chops, a bag of potatoes and a can of string beans. I can see him from the doorway, the back of his head as he sits in the easy chair watching television.

He comes back in while I'm emptying the beans into a pot. 'I like them rare,' he says and bends down to pull out the broiler.

'Don't you trust me?'

'My wife used to burn them. Every time. "What you got against the poor lamb?" I used to ask her, but it was me she was burning.'

I turn my back on him and begin stirring the beans.

'You mad?' He touches my back. I shrug him off, him and his wife talk. 'Listen. It's the first time since she left that I have a woman in my kitchen. Can you understand?'

He puts his arm across my chest and pulls me back from the stove still with the fork in my hand. 'I'm an old man. An old man gets cranky. He doesn't take to new ways.'

'You're not so old.'

'Thank you. You put it so delicately. Makes me feel so good.'

I turn in his arms and nudge him in the soft of his belly.

'I've still got my horns.' He pulls me back. 'Have we got time?'

'No. The lamb chops will burn and then you'll say.'

'You know what I love about you, you've got such a literal mind.'

I'm lying across his body, my face in his chest, my hands feeling his shoulders, his arms.

'You know I think we should go public,' he says.

I dig my face deeper in his chest.

'You hear? I think we should stop sneaking around.'

I move off him and lay back in the darkness.

'I don't know.'

'It's not natural. People got to know about us sometime.'

'Maybe. But not yet.'

'I'm tired of it. Every place we go you're looking behind us. We can't go uptown cause that's your family's turf. It's got to come out sometime.'

'You have to understand I could lose everything.'

'You don't think I've got something to lose?'

'Not as much as me.'

'You think just cause you're a white woman, people will say

54

"Caleb you've got a good thing". You think they won't say "What you doing Caleb hanging around some white bitch who you should only be balling?" "White meat" they'll say "is not tasty for long".'

But he said that I was not really white, no Jew is. 'Not someone with dun-colored nipples.'

'So when do you want to go public? You want to ride up to the Bronx now and knock on my mother's door? Take your white meat to the market.'

'That's not what I meant, you know that. I just want us to act natural.'

One day I went to the school from his house. On the platform at 125th Street I felt groggy and kept opening up my coat to make sure I had clothed myself. In the classroom I felt him dripping down my thighs. I ran to the bathroom and for a moment when I saw brown stains on my underpants and legs, I thought even his seed is colored. Then I realized that he had brought on my period.

'You see I'm giving a reading down in the village and I want you to come. I want to show you off.'

Caleb wears what he calls his 'poet's disguise': a black turtleneck, dungarees and a vest of rough white wool he picked up in Paris. He reads with a jazz band who plays stretched out notes between his lines and what sounds like tuning up between the stanzas.

I blush as I watch him on the small lighted stage, performing in public all the gestures I have begun to know, his hand outstretched offering the very air as a gift, the tipped palm which says 'if that's what you want to believe, if that's what you really want'. His body does a slow dance as he reads like an Indian I once saw perform on television, arching his back, then crouching, his face thrust forward so that the audience feels they cannot look away. I'm so embarrassed I stare at the floor until I feel him upon me, feel him pull me on the stage and then I raise my face and look at him only at him.

After the first set Caleb tries to make his way to me but people keep stopping him, at every table he passes hands draw his face down for a kiss, hold his arm till he drinks a coffee they ordered for him. I pretend not to understand when he sits down with a group and beckons to me. When he finally reaches me it is almost time for the second set. His throat is so dry from talking that he fears his voice might break.

They stare at me, the women from the other tables. They want to know everything about me for I have done what they only thought about in their white man's arms. I have seen their hands reaching up to him; I have seen that he could have them all after he reads, that they keep touching him as if his skin is magical. From all sides they stare at me while the men turn their backs to watch Caleb read again.

'It was so sensitive,' the man is saying, leaning over me to speak to Caleb. 'So sensitive. You know what I'm saying?'

'This is Sonia.' Caleb grasps my arm.

'Yes, hello dear.' The man looks down at me for a moment. His small face is nearly covered in beard and dry crinkly hair which grows low over his forehead. Only his large red lips like a wet lily seem alive.

'She's my inspiration,' Caleb says.

The man turns towards me again, gives me a close look as if he is trying to discover what he missed. Then he says to Caleb, 'When are you going to give me some poems? I've been waiting.'

'Yeah well I'm sorry, I've been busy.'

'I'm counting on you. We'll leave some blank spaces for you in the next issue.'

After he walks away, Caleb says, 'What a pain in the ass! He runs this magazine which about five people read, all of them himself.'

'So aren't you going to give him anything?'

'You must be kidding.'

'But what about the blank spaces?'

'That's bullshit. Blank spaces. Those are for his own crappy poetry.'

For once I do not have to rush off on Sunday to avoid his daughter who always comes across from Brooklyn to visit. The first time he said, 'Stay, stay. She's got to meet you sometime.' When I explained that I would feel uncomfortable, he shrugged his shoulders. Yet he did not ask me again. I know he does not want me to meet his daughter. I cannot imagine the two of us in the same room together, the solemn girl in the frame, a caricature of Caleb, the two of us on the couch with him watching.

But on this Sunday the girl is going to her friend's sweet sixteen party. Caleb keeps the shades lowered so that the morning lasts through the noon hour and the singing in the church next door. It's after three when we emerge from his apartment. We take a bus down to Times Square, stroll around looking for a movie, but there is nothing we both want to see.

'Let's have a bite,' Caleb says.

We begin walking up Broadway looking into the windows of delis and coffeeshops most of them closed or forsaken with waitresses leaning on the counters watching the street.

'Where is everybody?' Caleb asks.

If I were home my parents would be sipping glasses of lemon tea, my brother Leo sitting at the table drinking his from a soup dish because he can't wait for it to cool down.

A cold damp wind blows against our backs, the air tasting of snow. I notice the restaurant on the corner where I went so many years ago with my brother and pull Caleb across the street.

Still like a fairy's bedroom with make-believe snow in the windows, pink satin drapes in the entrance, a room of pink walls edged in shiny white, large gilt mirrors, and the moist sweet air of a florist.

'At least it's warm in here,' Caleb says.

The maître d' stands by a small table covered with a pink tablecloth watching us cross the white carpet.

'Do you think we should've taken our shoes off?'

'Shush,' I say. I know it was a mistake coming in here but too late to leave. The maître d' gathers up two menus, holds out his hand to guide us to a table.

'This place reminds me of something, I'm not sure what,' Caleb says.

It is as if we plunged in a newly made bed with all the dirt of the world on us. The maître d' leads us down the black marble stairs to a dimly lit room of empty tables covered with pink tablecloths, grey and black marble walls, mirrors too dark for reflection. He hands me an enormous white menu tied with pink ribbons, inside the food in small print on pink tissue paper pages.

'This is better. Upstairs was like a body turned inside out. You know those pictures in biology books of the organs? Everything pink and white except for the gall bladder. The gall bladder is always green.'

'You're talking so loud,' I whisper for the waiter lurks in the corner of the room.

'There's nobody here.' He opens the menu. 'They've got all this.' He waves his hands towards the mirrors, the marble walls. 'And then you look at the food.'

He begins to read from the pink pages as if they contain poetry. '"Grilled beefsteak with golden french fries, grilled grade A choice beef frankfurter, turkey club with garnish. Side orders: cole slaw, hearts of lettuce, Boston baked beans." We could've gone to the Automat.'

'I was here a long time ago.'

'Oh yeah. Can you recommend anything? What about a heart of lettuce?'

The waiter comes over and looks down at me. Caleb says, 'We haven't decided. You've got such a choice.'

'It's not his fault,' I whisper, 'Look. Do you want to go somewhere else?'

'Just relax will you? Ever since we came in here you've been tiptoeing around like you're walking on eggs.'

I close my menu. 'I'm going to have a hamburger.'

Caleb beckons to the waiter but the tall gaunt man remains at the far end of the room. Only when I look around at him does he begin to make his way towards us. He seems old enough to have been the one who embarrassed me by asking to cut my tomato. I remember that he did not smile when he saw my confusion but remained aloof.

'Actually,' Caleb says leaning over the table after the waiter disappears into the shadows. 'I'll tell you what it really reminds me of. When we came in the door, I thought it was just like being inside a woman only without the mirrors, the mirrors are inside your mind.'

He is trying to embarrass me.

'What's the matter with you anyway? Don't you like seeing a colored man in here?'

I am a child again shutting my eyes to keep the tears in while I eat.

He shakes the ketchup bottle hard but nothing comes out. He begins pounding the end till the red sauce suddenly leaps from the bottle and floods his french fries. 'Jesus! Why did I let you drag me in here?'

The gods are laughing at us, the gods who put such a quantity of tears in my eyes that I have to use my hands to staunch the flood.

'Why is it always you who gets hurt? Eh woman?'

'Don't call me woman.'

'Aren't you a woman? Or are you so above that?'

'Just don't call me woman like that.' I am breathing hard, my scalp prickly with anger.

'What do you want me to call you? Princess? Queen? Or would you prefer Miss Sonia?'

We walk separately up Broadway; I am like a nomad in the desert bereft of all my possessions. He heads east and I follow at a distance, lose him for a time in the crowds at Fifth Avenue, then see his bare dark head above the others, moving forward against the tide from the north. I try to keep him in sight without running to him but suddenly he disappears again and I am pushed to the edge of the sidewalk.

Caleb comes from behind to grab my arm. 'Just stay with me woman and you won't get lost.'

At Rockefeller Center, we push through the crowds to watch a lone skater below twirl self-consciously on the ice. When my brothers brought me here, Leo had to hoist me on his shoulder so I could see the figure skaters in their pink skirts and white tights. At first I thought it was a show, but then he told me that anyone could skate down there. Julius said how expensive it was but I knew he was afraid people would laugh at us.

The lone skater is joined by another more confident one who skates backwards and two little girls on trainer skates who walk across the ice.

'You wanna go down there?' Caleb asks.

'But we don't have skates.'

'Maybe we can rent.'

'But I haven't been skating for years.'

'Neither have I. But it comes back.'

'No I just couldn't.'

'Why? Just what are you afraid of?' He draws back from me with a wary look.

I grab his coat. 'It's not that. It's just that I'd feel like a fool falling while everyone was looking.'

'Everyone falls,' he whispers and kisses my ear. He takes my hand. 'Come on. We'll be like two bears.'

He pulls me out of the crowd around the railing and is searching for a way down, when I see them. Julius and Norma buying chestnuts for their daughter.

'Quick,' I say, 'Let's go.'

'What's the matter?'

'My brother.'

'I'm not moving,' he says.

But it is too late. My niece has seen me, is tapping her mother on the shoulder. The family comes towards us, square little people with the girl dancing backwards and forwards on her father's arm. They have seen his hand on mine, but in the twilight they cannot see me blushing.

Caleb has his hand out before I have even begun to introduce everyone. Julius looks startled but takes the hand. What else can he do? His face grows somber as he talks to the two of us. Norma gives Caleb questioning looks as if she can't quite decide if he is real. Jennifer hides behind her mother's coat when Caleb bends down to speak to her. Only when she thinks it safe to come out does she interrupt the adults to demand a chestnut. She juggles it until it is cool enough to eat. Caleb watches her struggle to pull open the shell.

'Let me help. I'm an expert.' He opens the nut so that the kernel emerges whole. She takes it from him but does not eat it. I see her throw the kernel on the ground when she thinks the grown-ups aren't looking.

When we separate, Julius and Norma taking the girl to see the skaters and the tree, Julius turns around and calls to me: 'Maybe we'll see you next Sunday.'

I mouth the words: 'Don't tell them you saw me.'

His face is sad. He shakes his head and I do not know if this means he can not read my lips or he is saying, 'What can I do after what you have done?'

9

Helen

Sheila made friends with me again. She saw me sitting on the edge of my group, not talking to anyone, chewing my Chicken à la King like it was the bitter herbs we ate at Passover.

'Hi moonface.' She hit me on the back, her pudgy face suddenly in my eye territory. 'What happened to you?'

'Nothing.' I wouldn't give in that easy. I continued to fork and chew.

'That stuff's disgusting,' she said, 'I threw mine away. Besides I'm on a diet.'

I couldn't believe this. Only the girls I hung around with went on diets; one of them goes to the bathroom everyday after lunch and sticks her finger down her throat. But Sheila wore her flesh like armor. Whenever I looked at her she had her hand in a bag of potato chips.

'Really. The doctor said no more sundaes. So I said what about Mondays?'

'Very funny.' But I stopped eating and turned my head up to talk to her. She knew she was back with me again, that the skinny girls with their faces like smiling hawks, their hands pulling and picking at each other across the narrow lunch table, would not even notice I had left them.

She asked me for that afternoon but I didn't want to lose my time with the photographs. I had become weird about them. Everyday I would come straight home from school, wait for my mother to go out shopping before I laid them out again on my parents' bed like paper dolls. I got nervous each time I opened the felt purse; maybe my mother had found out and replaced the photos with others of her and my father, so I would never be sure I'd really seen the black man. It was like the movie I once saw on television where the young bride goes up to the top room of a castle at midnight to find her husband's face in the mirror, but instead sees her own, now old and wrinkled. And yet each time I looked at the photos I got the same feeling as the first time, like opening up a report card and seeing a column of failures. My mother in the picture was a woman I didn't know, not the proud face I used to watch before the mirror, not even her. She looked satisfied as if the man had filled her with himself.

And then she sits there silently while my father lectures me about not marrying a black. 'You'd have such a hard time,' he says, not that he's prejudiced. 'It's like marrying a drug addict, you're looking for trouble.'

Like there's a chance one of them would even go out with me. They all sit together in the lunchroom. I got friendly with a black girl in my homeroom and made a fool out of myself by following her with my tray to their table. I was new so I didn't know. She looked so miserable because she couldn't tell me not to sit there and I couldn't just leave. So I sat on the edge of the group, but even there I heard the comments: 'I don't hate all whites. Don't you? No, only the ones look like they're still sucking their mother's tits.'

Shelia said what about Friday afternoon, a walk around the reservoir and then we'll take the bus to Fordham Road and have a soda. I preferred the Saturday when my mother was home all day cleaning, but Shelia was going shopping with her mother. I couldn't imagine her as somebody's daughter.

From the windows of my math class you can see the birds flying towards the reservoir, great crowds of black and white seagulls moving across the dull sky. Our eyes turn from the board where Mr. Landau is drawing an isosceles triangle. Does he sense we're no longer paying attention, that we're with the birds who suddenly turn and head straight for the high windows of our room? But this is only to tease us for they swoop near, then fly above the building.

Shelia keeps falling out of her high heels so we walk slowly around the reservoir. I stare at the water while she talks. The sky has cleared and all the light of the day fallen into the water, so bright that when I turn away I see white flashes in the air. We sit down on a bench in the little strip of park which surrounds the reservoir. She's talking about her new boyfriend. There's a secret she can only tell to me. I figure she has gone all the way. She slips back against the bench and I'm halfway turned facing her.

A man comes down the path and sits with us. 'Good afternoon girls,' he says.

Shelia keeps her back to him, rolls her eyes and says nothing. I don't like the look of him. He's all the time smiling but his broad shiny face looks afraid as if he's guilty and trying to make amends. I turn away from Sheila and stare at the water while she talks.

She's saying she can't even tell her mother though they're like sisters, even her mother would get upset and cry.

Maybe I know as I stare at the water that something is happening, that the man's eyes never leave us, that he watches Sheila jiggle her legs. Maybe out of the corner of my eyes I see what he's doing. But I keep staring at the water till I'm nearly blind and Sheila's words come at me like echoes.

'Why?' I ask.

'I just told you why. Aren't you even listening to me? He's black, my boyfriend.'

She punches my shoulder. I look back at her and see a fountain coming from the man's pants, his face pleading with me as if to say he can do nothing, the shiny rubbery thing has a life of its own.

'Let's go,' I say. Sheila looks at me hard, then gets up without saying a word. She doesn't even turn around to see him. I hear her stumbling behind me as I run down the path.

'Wait up will you?' she says. 'He's not following.'

I don't stop running till we reach the street. She has to take off her shoes to keep up with me.

'You didn't see,' I say. 'I'm the one.' I'm crying, beating my fists against my side. She puts her arm around me. I feel her heat, smell the perfumed sweat as I cry against her.

'You've never seen one?'

I turn my head from side to side against her shoulder.

'I know it looks disgusting the first time. You think "that's not going up me".'

I pull away from her and stand alone in the street, my back hunched.

'C'mon. We'll get a soda. I'll treat.' She hits me lightly on the shoulder, but I don't budge. She takes my hand and drags me along, drags me all the way down the Grand Concourse. I don't know what people think seeing us holding hands like we're lessies. I feel like someone put blinders on me and all I can see is the sidewalk ahead of me; if I shift my eyes to one side I'm in speckled darkness which only her hand can guide me through.

10

Sonia

Nightfall, The Museum III

The chest a black petal, perfection but
for a chipped eyelid, the excavator struggling
to possess, the earth resisting, his hands, the blade slips.
His look of readiness, spear grasped as if
he hears crowds stamping through the city
smells wolves descending.

Julius picks me up from school and drives slowly through the
back streets downtown. He says he happened to be in the area but I
know it has all been planned; he talked to his wife, then sat alone
in the livingroom with his small fingers pressing his forehead
thinking through my case. He asks if we can stop for coffee, that
way he'll miss the rush hour going out to Queens. Even this has
been planned, the excuse I can't refuse, the treat of cake and coffee
with my favorite brother.

He's wearing his lawyer's outfit, the navy blue suit, the matching
tie like a tunnel down his white shirt. 'You're coming to my funeral
already?' my father used to say.

He parks with the anxious look of a man squeezing himself into
a narrow space, though there is plenty of room for his car, and takes
my arm as we cross the street, a reflex from when I was his little
sister. But now he looks like a small boy next to me and when he
takes my coat in the coffeeshop, I think he staggers from the weight
and size of it.

'Whatever will be will be.' Someone begins feeding the jukebox
with Doris Day.

I want to sit at the counter, but he takes me to a corner booth.

'It's quieter here,' he says.

'Have something,' he urges when I order coffee. 'A piece of pie. They have your favorite.'

When I tell him I'm not hungry, he looks hurt. I feel sorry for him then, for the boy face behind the frameless glasses and the worry creases, all his fun gone. He used to play tricks on Leo, the two of us conspiring against his tyranny. I was his little helper; I'd crawl under the table and tickle Leo's legs and then while he tried to grab me, Julius would steal his plate. Once Julius set all the alarm clocks and we hid them in Leo's room. Just as Leo discovered and turned off one clock, another across the room would begin its siren. He danced back and forth like a caged bear while we laughed.

'So how's your class going?'

'They're okay. Not the brightest I've ever had.'

'What about that girl you told me about? The one who was such a problem.'

'You mean Christine?' No one else in the family remembered such details. 'She's not the problem. It's the others picking on her.'

'But she sounds a little crazy.'

'Maybe she is. But then wouldn't you be if everyone was ganging up on you all the time? If you felt like a misfit?'

'I guess so.' Does he remember the times Leo picked the boys off of him? Leo smiling, holding his brother at the back of the neck like a cat as they came in the door. Julius would shake him off, rush into the bathroom and lock the door behind him. Beneath the sound of water I heard sobbing. I made my doll knock at the door but he did not answer. When he finally emerged, I followed him around the house until he turned and said sadly, 'What do you want with me?'

The waitress, a tall gaunt elderly woman with a weary face, clears the table and puts down paper mats. Her movements are slow and accompanied by sighs. She drops a spoon, sighs yet again and whispers, 'The show must go on.'

Julius waits for her to leave before beginning. He clasps his hands on the edge of the table. 'So are you seeing anyone?'

I smile, nod my head but will give him no entrance.

'You're not talking?'

'What are you asking?'

'It's not the man we met you with?'

I have tried to keep myself inside, I have tried to be the Sonia they know but suddenly I am flushed with anger at his calm, reasonable manner. 'He has a name you know.'

'I'm sorry. Everything was so quick I forgot. What is it?'

I want to slap him, his neutral lawyer face which once cried so easily. 'Never mind,' I say.

'What are you getting angry for? All I asked.'

I stand up. He reaches across the table. 'Please Sonia. Can't we talk about this like civilized people?'

I watch him turn around to make sure no one is listening, frightened that even these strangers should know about me. I sit down again. He is pitiful.

'It's just that I'm concerned.'

I pretend not to understand. 'About what?'

'Well. Is it serious?'

'Is what serious?'

'You know what I'm talking about Sonia. Please. I'm trying to help.'

'Have you told everyone else?'

'No. I was waiting to talk to you.'

The waitress sets down our cups with a clumsy flourish so that coffee spills over the rims. 'It's not my fault,' she wails and hurries away.

Julius shakes his head as if to say this is always happening to him, lifts the saucer and pours the excess coffee into his cup. I let mine slosh around, so that every time I lift my cup, he says, 'Watch it Sonia, you're dripping.' Such a whiner he is.

'It must be serious,' he concludes, 'Or you wouldn't get so mad.' He watches me as he speaks but I have made my face a sullen mask. I will not bear witness.

'You'll give Pop such aggravation.'

'So don't tell him.'

'But if it's serious.' He is hoping that if I really consider his question, I will see the truth and the colored man will fade from my mind.

'Listen Sonia, you know I'm not narrow-minded. It's just that it would be so hard for you. It's like marrying a mentally ill person. You don't want to take on his problems for the rest of your life.'

'Who said anything about marrying?'

'I'm just saying "If". I mean he seemed very nice but there other men. Jewish men. You know that. You're just being stubborn.'

I want to say 'leave me alone, leave me and forget you ever saw him'. He is ruining it for me, making Caleb part of his dull world.

'In fact Norma knows a friend who wants to fix you up with someone, a professor I think. If you just say the word.' He smiles at me. She'll come around, he's thinking, it is just a question of saying the right things. You have to be careful with Sonia, she can be so contrary. No point in making threats.

'What do you say?' he asks.

'I'm not interested.' When Julius was in college one of his classmates came around to ask him to join the Communist party. My mother was crying in the shadows; she did not even want him to invite the boy in so afraid she was of the house being tainted. When he shut the door I ran from him, from the stink of fear in his breath, even the hands he held out to me: Sonia, Sonia darling what's the matter? I was only a kid so what did I know?

'You want to ruin your life?'

I feel nothing, am as pure and cold as the polar wastes behind the glass window of the museum. A Negro man stands beside me laughing at Julius's small life in the small rooms where his wife fries latkes and wipes finger marks from the furniture.

'Okay then. Okay if that's what you want.' But still I do not speak and he realizes he has lost his ally. I see through the frost which has settled around me that he is afraid he might cry there in the bright coffeeshop and lowers his head, makes fists to contain his tears.

'You can blab to everyone,' I say, 'I don't care.'

69

He looks up at me, his face pale from having to hold back. 'Since when did I ever tell on you?'

❊ ❊ ❊

'What would they say if I came? Eh? To your bloodletting?' Caleb holds me around the waist. I am trying to dress and turn and push against his arms.

'Bloodletting? What are you talking about?'

'You know the stories about Jews sacrificing Christians on Passover, leaching the blood from little boys like the angel of death.'

'That's vicious.' I break away.

'I know all about it. You're not the first Jew I've been with.'

I remember the white hands reaching up to him, the looks from the women, not envy, but curiosity. I have been a fool.

'Don't look so shocked. One of them even took me home to your feast. She said they would speak English part of the time but everything was in Hebrew. Sometimes I'd hear an English word, but so low I couldn't understand. Maybe they were afraid I'd steal their prayers from them. I was so bored I slipped out when they let the prophet in.'

'Just like that?'

'They were standing by the door calling him: "Elijah, Elijah". I figured they were hoping he'd take my place. Which he did.'

' What about your girlfriend?'

'She came running after me, but I never saw her again after that.'

'It was stupid of her to invite you.'

'I don't know. I think she was hoping I'd be accepted, that if her parents saw me at their table, they would realize I was human.'

'You know what my family would say. Who is that *shvartzer* you brought here?'

'What's that mean?'

'Didn't your other Jewish girlfriends tell you?' Once when I picked a bright orange coat from the rack at Macy's, my mother pulled it from me and whispered, 'You want to look like a *shvartzeh*?' *Shvartzer*. Everyone smirked when they said the word, as if it were dirty, a curse.

'It's like nigger then,' Caleb says and when I try to explain, 'Don't tell me. Jews.' He shakes his head. 'You're not like the other whites. No. You don't just rob our bodies but our souls.'

※ ※ ※

We always leave the door ajar on Passover eve, in case, my father used to say, the prophet wants to come early and stay for a meal. Julius said it was really for strangers to enter and be welcome but no one ever joined us.

When I push open the door, I nearly collide with my mother who is concentrating on carrying a soup bowl of salt water to the table. 'Ooh Sonia. Don't make me spill the Jewish tears.' She has already pulled out the leaves of the table, laid a white tablecloth, set down the other symbolic dishes. Always these were my jobs: to roast the chicken neck and egg over the blue gas flame, chop the apples and nuts, mix with honey and sweet red wine to make the Pharaoh's mortar, spoon out the red horseradish so each of us could taste the Jewish bitterness, and arrange them all like a surrealistic still life on the long shaky table.

When we sat down, opened our Haggadahs and my father began to bless the wine, I imagined hundreds of tiny Jews rushing about the table, building the Pharaoh's walls from my sweet mortar, dragging the chicken neck now become a bloody lamb's head across the doors of Jewish houses, cleaning the blood from their hands with water from the pitcher I had set down by my father, eating the matzos so quickly, for they were always on the run, that they choked on the bread of affliction and had to drink their own tears, then solemn faced, their children still crying, they crossed the soup bowl to wander for forty years in white linen desert. Over and over again they performed for me, oblivious to the high voice of Leo's son singing the four questions, to the tears on my father's face when he said, 'Next year in Jerusalem.'

'Where's Pop?' I walk into the living-room but the easy chair is empty.

'He wasn't feeling well. I told him to lie down.' We hear slow heavy steps, shoes scraping against the floor. The stroke left him with the walk of a hesitant giant. My mother looks down the hallway. 'Ah. There he is now. He must have heard you.'

I am uncomfortable as he kisses my forehead and he senses this and lets me go. I washed myself, but can still smell Caleb, still feel his thighs upon me.

We sit down on the sofa together. I wait for the questions to come out. Was I still happy in that apartment with the other girl? Did I never think of coming back to them?

Years ago my mother warned me not to make him angry by acting contrary, but now he has no temper to lose. Could he even remember what it was like to holler till Julius fled from the house without his dinner, to push Leo, a big boy of sixteen, across the room so he toppled and fell and cried in his mother's arms? And when the house was empty of sons, to sit in the easy chair letting the darkness settle over him like a caul. I would come out of the room I had hidden in during the shouting. At first when I touched him he did not stir. His large rough hand was limp when I picked it up. When I felt he was watching me, I held his wrist with both my hands and played the joke he always played on me. I made his hand slap against his knee. 'Stop hitting yourself Papa,' I'd say, 'Why do you want to do that for?'

It is Leo's Seder night. After his stroke, my father moved from the head to the side of the table, his speech too halting for him to lead. At first my brothers took turns but after Julius' daughter was old enough to ask the four questions, and thus supplanting Leo's boy, Leo complained it was too crowded at the table with both families, and they began to come on different nights.

Now there is no fool at the Seder. For years my brothers kicked each other under the table, let their yarmulkahs fall over their eyes, and demanded food while my father explained how we could tell we were free people just by the way we sat. My father ignored them, but once when Leo brought the soup bowl up to his mouth and pretended to slurp the salt water, he smacked him hard.

'Not the head,' my mother cried.

'Where else?' My father stood up from the table now drenched with salt water and left his wife to pick up the pieces of the soup bowl, to hold her big son who rocked from side to side clutching his forehead.

Now Leo sits in my father's chair flanked by his son and Pop. He has a disheveled look as if he is still the fool, but his manner is solemn as he lifts up the cloth from the matzos and announces: 'This is the bread of affliction which our forefathers ate in the land of Egypt.' He waves towards the door: 'All who are hungry let them come and eat.'

In the candlelight I watch the tiny Jews struggling with their burdens. I take great gulps of wine when I am told to raise my glass. The Seder will go on for another hour, the son chanting prayers in Hebrew while Leah smiles, my mother sneaking into the kitchen to make sure the potatoes do not burn, my father silent in his black jacket and satin yarmulkah.

'In every generation each person must look upon himself as if he personally had come out of Egypt.'

I sleep and wake, the little Jews crawling over my hands.

'We must never forget that she is surrounded by enemies.'

I wake from a doze, startled, my heart beating, my face burning from the wine.

'We thank God Israel has been returned to us but we must never be complacent.' He looks around the table as if to bring us back, his daughter rubbing at some stain on her sleeve, my mother half out of her chair again. What does he think as he hears my father mumbling some Hebrew prayer out of the corner of his mouth, does he imagine another stroke which will close his papa's lips?

I stare dreamily at the plates on the table. When we all stand up to let Elijah in, my legs are weak. I know Leo is watching me now, my rosy face, my sleepy eyes, my mouth half open as if I expect the prophet to come and embrace me.

My mother's soup chicken and carrot tsimmes and the soft red jello with the fruit sunk to the bottom do not restore me. I shut my eyes and the passage to the train station is awash with the Pharaoh's soldiers. I have missed God's crossing.

'Can you give me a lift home?' I am not on his way but Leah says, 'Take her first. By the time you get back we'll be finished with the dishes.'

'It's always a special moon on Passover,' I say, my head tipped back on the seat.

'Special to you.'

I hear him in the hollow of my brain, the cave my senses have left behind, his peevish voice an echo. He does not like to see my lips stained with wine. I have done as God requests, but he thinks I drank the four glasses to make him the fool again.

'Mom's worried about you,' he says.

I say nothing to this.

'Do you hear? She thinks you're gallivanting around.'

Mom stepping away from the door, lowering her voice: 'Do you think she brings men up there? It cannot be. No not our Sonia.'

'She's worried I tell you.'

'So. What else is new?' What does he care about what Mom thinks? He wants only to pull me from the fiery whirlwind. I shut my eyes and it lifts me out of the car up towards the yellow moon.

We pass under the train roar. 'Put up your window,' he says suddenly.

I open my eyes. Am blinded by the brilliance of the night city: red neon words above tents of light, cars flowing by like strange deep sea fish. Then I recognize the street where I first met the man with the newspaper. Soon we will pass within a few blocks of Caleb's house.

I am hot from the wine and unbutton my coat. 'Can't we open a window? It's so stuffy.'

'I'll turn off the heat.'

I squirm in the closed car, pull off my coat. The heat has traveled to my lap, if not for his eyes upon me I would touch myself.

'Please open the window.'

'What are you, crazy? This is a bad neighborhood.'

'Can't breathe.' I fumble with the door handle. By the time he pulls up at the curb, I have already pushed my legs out the door.

'Sonia!' he yells, 'What are you doing?'

74

'I have a colored man here.' My voice is thick, my mouth sour with sweet Jewish wine, blood smeared on the doors of the first born.

Leo pushes himself along the seat, tries to grab me, but cannot move fast enough; his flesh gets in his way, the belly he always jokes about. I grab my coat, trail it behind me as I run from him. He drives along the curb beseeching me to come in, for he is too afraid to leave the car to chase me. I lose him down some alleyway, some snaking river he cannot pass through. What will my mother say? 'I have a little sister, but I have lost her momma, lost her in a strange land where the buildings rise up like colored men.'

11

Helen

Sheila doesn't even tell me he's going to be there. She calls me up on Sunday morning to ask if I want to go to Central Park. My mother is still nervous about me going downtown alone but when I tell her I'll be meeting Sheila at Pelham Parkway and we'll take the subway together, she is all right about it.

I'm dying to get out. On Sundays my house is a morgue, with my father the stiff on the sofa reading the *Daily News*, my mother dragging around the house like a ghost in her pink and grey duster, me under the covers till noon when she comes in and pulls up the venetian blinds, and my father changes out of his bathrobe.

Till I'm outside I don't realize how sour the place smells. It's one of those bare early April days when even the soot tastes of perfume and all the time you're smelling something you can't have. It used to drive me crazy when I was a little kid. My mother said once I tried to eat the grass in Bronx Park. She thought I was imitating the goats I'd seen at the zoo, but it was the smell like the earth was cooking and I must have my portion.

Sheila is dressed trampy even for her: a red velour top with a deep V neck which shows off her bra, and jeans so tight, my father would say, 'you can see her ass cheeks'. I watch girls trying on pants in Alexander's, squeezing their flesh in, lying down on the floor to pull up the zipper and then parading triumphantly in front of the mirror with their thighs like water ballons. The women's libbers say we should dress to please ourselves, throw away the bras and girdles, but nobody's listening; they're still strapping themselves in like Scarlet O'Hara. I'm so thin everything hangs on me, 'Skinny galoot' they used to call me when I was little, just like my father before he got married and started spreading.

We get off at Fifty-Ninth Street and walk up through the park to Sheep's Meadow. The grass is still dry and brown from winter but you can see the green roots coming up. We bought some meatball subs near the subway and the tomato sauce is beginning to drip through the paper so I ask why don't we stop and eat, but she seems to have some destination in mind and wants to keep moving. I rip open the paper and begin eating while we walk.

I hear drumming, even the sound of a horn very low. Her head perks up and she changes direction. We're moving through bushes, sometimes walking into trees as she chases the sound.

'Where are you going anyway?' I still have half a sub in my hands. I'm having trouble eating it because she's moving so fast. When she doesn't answer, I say, 'I wanna know where we're going.'

She keeps walking till we reach the top of a hill and then she turns to me. 'Look. Do you want to come with me or not?'

I have an entire meatball in my mouth so all I can do is nod.

'So stop kvetching.'

The sounds grow louder as we pass through a grove of trees. I follow Sheila down the hill to a clearing where three black guys play the drums and a fourth blows on a saxophone. They have only the scatterings of an audience in the tall grass. We sit down on the slope of the hill, Sheila with her back straight, her chest stuck out, the zipper on her jeans bulging.

They sound confused as if each one is playing by himself. When the saxophone player puts down his horn, picks up a can of beer from the grass and wanders away, the others don't seem to notice.

'They're just practicing,' Sheila says. She keeps looking at one of the drummers but he is intent on the pounding his fists are giving the skin of his drum. He's maybe twenty but looks like an old style black. He doesn't have an Afro; his hair is what they call 'nappy', parted on the side and combed back like straightened steel wool from his forehead. He dresses cheap and gaudy: shiny purple shirt, black satiny bells on a body thin and quick as a fork of lightning.

One by one they stop playing. He is the last. You can see he's has something good going and can't bear to let it end. When he stops, he's the only one to look up at the people listening and get some applause but his surly face never relaxes into a smile. He's the kind of black I would move to the next subway car to escape from.

Sheila gets up to go to him but he makes a motion with his hand to say he'll come there. He kisses her on the mouth hard like he's marking her for his own. You see these couples on the subway, the boy clutching his girl close like she is his money.

When Sheila introduces me to Eddie, he gives me an unfriendly look. 'What's your sign?' he asks.

I don't even know but when I tell him my birthdate, he thinks for a moment, then says, 'You're Aries. That's a fire.' He looks even more unfriendly. 'I'm a Capricorn. Sheila's Taurus. We're both earth.'

The other guys saunter over with their drums. One of them, a beanpole type, very black with a gold tooth, crouches down in front of me and starts asking me where I hang out. Doesn't matter what I say, he smiles. I can see he has something else on his mind, and I begin to get scared.

'She's too young for you,' Eddie says.

'How old are you?' the beanpole asks.

'Fourteen. Just.'

'See what I mean,' Eddie says with a sneer.

I wonder what he's got against me. Maybe it's my sign.

Sheila is laughing though Eddie's face is dead serious. We're the same age only she's not too young. Eddie is crouched behind her now with his arm around her neck; he looks at me from behind her head like he wants me gone.

I want to leave but can't remember the way back for we zigzagged so much coming here. I figure we're on the west side of the park which is a foreign country to me.

While Eddie talks, Sheila watches me with an indulgent smile, like I'm her little daughter. She sees the beanpole still hovering around, making me nervous. I keep getting up, walking around with my hands in my pockets, then sitting down as far from him as possible.

'You got ants in your pants?' she calls out. Which is not helpful for it prompts the beanpole to say, 'Hey slow down girl, little girl.'

'I think I better go.' I have no hopes now that Sheila will leave with me. She's smoking and when Eddie lights up, they exchange cigarettes. Which seems silly because they're both smoking the same brand. But I see it's not just an ordinary exchange. Their faces are close and Eddie gives her a hard look.

I just have to hope that the beanpole doesn't follow and that I'll walk east not north into Harlem.

I see Sheila whispering to Eddie.

'But what about tonight?' he says pulling her towards him.

She shrugs her shoulders, tries to break free. 'I said tonight. I'm seeing you tonight.'

'I can't,' she says.

'I must have you tonight,' he whispers but everyone can hear. 'I must.' He pulls her even closer. She turns her head away when he tries to kiss her. This seems enough to discourage him for he loosens his arms. She staggers up, brushing the grass from her pants. He gets up quickly, his chest flung out, his face angry again. He's making sure she doesn't leave him sitting in the grass his face sour with disappointment.

'See you when I see you,' he says and walks over to the other guys who are starting to play again.

'He's mad at you,' I say as we walk away.

'He's always mad,' Sheila says, but she turns around to see if he's watching her, turns back with a smirk.

'I'm sorry if it was because of me.'

'Don't worry about it. I'm seeing him tomorrow night.' She has another look around. 'What do you think of him? Don't you think he's fine?'

He's a nightmare, why is she going out with a nightmare?

'Black boys are the best,' she says.

We can hear them drumming again and the weak notes of the saxophone. I think about the photos in the felt purse of the black man but can't say anything to Sheila for it's a secret I robbed from my mother.

Somehow she finds the way back to the east side of the park before the darkness settles over us, Sheila who has such a bad sense of direction that she gets lost in the lunchroom.

But even so I get home late, hours after my parents already have their dinner. We always eat at 6 o'clock. My father likes to have his supper on the table as soon as he gets home from work. Sundays are no different.

There's a lone plate on the table but nobody is around the kitchen. I walk through the livingroom and down the hall shouting my 'hellos' till I reach the back room, my parents' bedroom. They turn from the window, my father all goggle-eyed.

'Where were you?' my mother demands.

They have been watching for me, hoping to see me wandering down the street from the subway.

'We were ready to call the police,' my father says, 'You don't do that again you hear? You got us so worried.'

'Where were you?' my mother keeps asking.

'I told you. I met Sheila, then we went to the park.'

'We let you go downtown yourself and look what happens.'

'Nothing happened. Sheila's mother lets her go downtown all the time.'

'I don't care what Sheila's mother does.' My mother hates to be compared with anyone.

My father pipes in: 'Isn't she divorced?' When I nod my head he says, 'Well that explains it.'

My mother gives him a scornful look but he doesn't notice. 'You call us next time you're going to be late. We'll pick you up,' he says.

He's really going to come for me in the middle of Central Park, save me from some black beanpole with a gold tooth. He can't even imagine where I've been.

But I'm relieved for when I didn't find anyone in the kitchen or livingroom, when I heard their voices in the back room, I thought they'd found out I'd been playing with my mother's photos. Maybe I had not been careful enough about returning the felt purse to the right place in my mother's sweater drawer. I don't know what I'm afraid of. They've caught me nosing around their room before. I used to play with the buttons in my mother's sewing box and try on her sealskin coat. And hadn't my mother read the sex parts of my diary, then with an embarrassed face told me my language was dirty.

'What do you mean?' I asked, knowing what she had done. But she wouldn't confess.

I don't want them to know I know. Sheila said once when she was little, she had a nightmare and ran into her parents' bedroom. All she remembered was lots of shiny skin and her father yelling at her to get out. But it wouldn't be like that for me. They would cover themselves and we would all have to pretend it never happened.

12

Sonia

Nightfall, The Museum IV

He seems, yes is warm
from summer penetrating even these walls,
or from the hands of the furtive
While the guard dreams, Coney Island rising beyond shut eyes
I touch his thighs, smooth like a young boy's
We lie down together, still
he holds his spear, as if it had become part of him.

'You're paranoid,' Caleb says, 'Nobody even notices us. Why should they?'

But it is only in the Village that I feel comfortable holding hands in public with Caleb. For everyone is queer down here. On Sunday we stroll with the normal people who come down from the hills of Bronx and the plains of Long Island to stare at the women with their breasts hanging free under their turtlenecks, the men with hair like bird's nests and baggy sweaters smelling of sweat and tobacco. 'Disgusting,' they whisper but cannot stop themselves looking and looking.

'How did they get that way?' The normal people wonder to each other. The young men and women lolling on the street, whose lives seem inside out.

Yet they find themselves acting strangely, pointing and staring at people when they taught their children not to be so rude, not to court danger. They crowd into little stores selling earrings and bangles, clay pots and Spanish tiles, and buy things they do not need for their coffee tables: misshapen ashtrays, rough red nut bowls they are pleased to tell their friends came from the Village. They eat their hamburgers in coffeeshops so dark, they joke, you need a flashlight to read the menu, and have their children's faces drawn by street artists whose names they soon forget.But their children never forget. Leo's girl dressed as a beatnik on Halloween, making squares in the air when he tells her to turn off the bellyaching she calls music.

I notice people's eyes on me, those who have had a surfeit of the disheveled young people on the street and see in the two of us a piquant treat. Down here we are royalty. Artists call out to Caleb that they will do his portrait for free, such a fine head he has. Sometimes a cafe owner recognizes him and asks if he could read a poem that evening.

Once a photographer, a small Jewish man with a grey goatee and shaggy brows, a head too big for his elfin body, dragged us over to Washington Square and took us standing beneath a tree. First it was me and Caleb and then Caleb alone and I knew it was Caleb he wanted all along, Caleb hugging the fork of a bare young tree, eyes gleaming in the bitter sunlight.

'We don't have to go, do we? Not yet,' I say. So we have a bite to eat at one of the dark hamburger joints. When he asks for the check I want to say do I have to go home now do I? He sees the look in my eyes and says okay baby you stay another night. We stop at my apartment so I can get my school clothes and books.

Irene lounges in the doorway of her bedroom watching me make Caleb coffee in the kitchen. She's in her bathrobe, her face dim without makeup, only her mouth, a smudge of red shows she cares what we think. 'I haven't talked to anyone in two days,' she says.

'Where's Harvey?'

'He's selling in Chicago. To hog butchers.'

But I've heard the joke before. Harry's always going to Chicago.

'Are you still writing poetry?' she asks Caleb.

'Why still?'

'Even poets get tired. I have a friend who says she's written out.'

'You mean I'm past it?'

'Don't be so touchy. I heard you read a couple of years ago. You were so good, I remembered you. You had a certain something.'

'Is that supposed to be a compliment?'

83

'I don't know how you stand it,' Irene calls out to me but I walk deeper into my closet, pretend not to hear.

'Maybe you could read for my group. We've got an evening coming up on civil rights. We've got someone who was in on the bus boycott in Montgomery.'

'Only my poetry is not about civil rights.'

'Doesn't matter. If you could just give us a poem or two, it would be perfect.'

He walks into my room. 'You ready?'

I laid two dresses on the bed, am trying to decide which one.

'Just give me a minute.'

'You want me to choose?'

'What's your hurry?'

Caleb sits down on the bed. 'Your girlfriend's got a viper tongue and viper eyes.'

'Shush. She can hear you.'

'She want everyone to taste her poison.'

'Can't you whisper? She's just being friendly. What do you want her to do when you come over, disappear?'

'You think maybe she is actually flirting with me?'

'Look what you made me do.' I hold up a stocking so he can see the run. 'You're making me crazy. We'll never get out of here.'

'Okay, I get the message.' He returns to the kitchen but I don't hear anymore talk between them. When I come out with my little red case packed, the curtain is drawn across the entrance to her room and I can hear her shuffling around her furniture.

I call out 'Irene' but she says nothing. Has stopped her ears. She left me, she spent whole weekends cocooned with Harvey in her room. 'Irene, I'm going back to Caleb's.' Again nothing. She can't stand for me to be the one. 'I'll see you at school.' She says something back but her words are muffled by the purple curtain and the sounds of the radio.

I have not thought about what we would do with the rest of the evening in his apartment. Usually we have a plan, supper out and a movie, or we meet late and only have time for a coffee and bed.

Caleb declares that Sunday is his night to lounge and he eases himself in a chair before the television, his legs apart, his hands resting on the bolsters as if he were in a movie theater. I come and sit on his lap, but he is so absorbed that when I move he looks down at me as if surprised to see me in his arms. I stand up, go round the back of his chair and lean against him.

'What are you watching?'

'Some old movie.'

'Don't you even know what you're watching?'

'It started already. I'll find out after the commercial.'

'But you're watching anything. Just to watch.'

'I'm relaxing. Tomorrow people will be pestering me with questions again.'

'But. . .'

'Shush Sonia.'

I wander away, pick up the pictures of his daughter and mother from his desk, cross the room in front of the television.

'Come on,' he complains, 'You're getting in the way.'

I part the curtains to look at the dark form of the church, then let them drop and begin to pace behind his chair till he says, 'What's with you? Can't you find something to do?'

I lie down on the sofa, very still with my feet tucked under me, my cheek against the hard arm. I could be back home with pop reading *The Forward*, Mom watching *Ed Sullivan*; only I am waiting for Caleb to turn off the television, come over to me after I have shut my eyes and carry me into the bedroom.

But when the movie ends, he walks by me into the kitchen. I hear the refrigerator open and close, a bottle top being wrenched off, a knife hitting a cutting board.

'You want anything to eat?' he calls out.

'No.' But I speak with my mouth in the sofa and he does not hear.

'I said, "do you want anything?"' He stands in the kitchen doorway.

'I said "no".'

'What's the matter with you?'

'Nothing.'

'Then stop sulking. It doesn't become you.'

He sits down at his desk with a bottle of beer and a sandwich. I pretend to doze off on the sofa, but I am watching him.

'Aren't you going to sleep?' I ask.

'You go. I'm working on something.'

'One of your poems?'

'Maybe.'

'Is it a new one?

'Too soon to say. It's bad luck.'

Is it coming out of him now, twisting its way through his belly?

I sit on the hard chair by his bed reading but all the time listening to him sigh in the next room, to the scratch of his fountain pen. I undress and crawl into the bed, vast and empty compared to the one my parents share, switch off the lights and hope for once I can sleep through the night. Always I am aware of the dark head beside me, of the powerful curve of his back as he sleeps with the pillow bunched in his arms, of his legs loose beside me, of the yeasty smell we make together, of the words which come out of him even in his dreams. I sleep for minutes, then wake with a start as if by sleeping at all I have lost something: Caleb gone from my side and me back in my old bed in my parents' house. Never the narrow one in the coffin room, for which I pay rent, never do I dream myself in that bed stained with blue light, even though it is there I spend most of my nights.

I am swimming from the grassy shore, from the old man on the park bench who cries out, 'It is forbidden,' to an island where no one has ever lived. There in the middle of a land dry and grey as concrete is an ancient building with the word 'museum' carved in the arched doorway. Inside, one of embalmed bodies mounted on blocks of stone like statues begins to breathe again, his sighs terrible to hear as he presses himself upon me, his body like warm clay, his smell of sour wine.

'You awake?' Caleb rolls me over and I can taste the beer.

❋ ❋ ❋

86

'We haven't told Mom yet,' Leo says over the phone.

The two brothers joined together after all these years to talk about me. I can hear the phone calls between Yonkers and Queens, the wives drawing close, Norma whispering, 'Don't get involved. What do you want to get involved for? He's only trying to use you. If your sister wants to ruin her life, let her.'

Leah standing before Leo as he dials his brother. 'Make sure he says something too. Why should you always be the bad one?'

'Is that a threat?' I say. I've pulled the phone in from the kitchen, am lying across the sofa in Irene's room, my feet touching the pile of clothes she's spent the last hour selecting for tomorrow, the first day of open school week. Irene sets up her ironing board in front of the radio.

'No of course not. It would upset her so much, what's the point?'

'So why tell me you haven't told her?'

'You know why Sonia. You're just being childish.'

'You don't have to insult me. If you're going to insult me, I'm getting off.'

'Somebody has to tell you. We've always given into you. All your crazy romantic ideas. But this is too much. Think what you would be doing if you married the guy. Where would you even live?'

'There are places.'

'Where? Where would they accept both of you?'

'There's the Village.'

'Nobody lives in the Village. Only creeps.'

I notice they call on alternate nights and present different arguments, but both assume this colored man whose name they never mention wants to bind me in marriage. It never occurs to them that he might not want me that way, that he has never even proposed, that Caleb would laugh if I even mentioned the word.

Last night it was Julius: 'Have you thought about his people? How would they take to you? Have you even thought about that?'

I thought of the daughter I refused to meet and lied to him. 'I've met them.'

'And?'

'And everything's fine.'

'I'm sure they're fine people but you'll discover in the end that they won't accept you and then where will you be?'

'I'll have you.'

Silence on the other end of the phone.

'Wouldn't I?'

'Maybe you'd have me but I don't know about anyone else.'

Irene finishes her ironing and drapes her slip, a white blouse and blue suit on the back of the easy chair. The radio is turned down but I hear the grunts of Elvis Presley: 'You get me so lonely. You get me so lonely I could die.'

When I put down the phone, I cannot move from my position prone on the sofa. The shadows of the furniture in the big room have taken on flesh.

'Have you told Caleb what's happening?' Irene asks.

'No. I don't want him to know.'

'He's got to find out sometime your family's waging war against him.'

'Not my whole family.'

'You don't think your parents would have conniption fits if they found out?'

'Look, do you think you could turn that off for a minute. It's giving me a headache.'

'What do they see in him?' Irene says. 'My niece is crazy about him. She called up her friend one night he was on radio and just screamed into the phone. And the friend knew of course who it was and why. One follows the other. They've got no mind of their own.'

'Just turn it off.' But it is Irene's harsh voice I want to silence. I bury my face in one of the hard little throw pillows.

'Something funny happened today at school,' Irene is saying, 'You want to keep this under your hat.'

I am having a conversation in my head with Leo and Julius. I explain and explain and they begin to nod their heads. Even so some dread takes possession of me, no matter how I shape my words, how they bend to me, the dread comes back and back.

'I tell you you're not the only one with problems. Miss Booth called me into her office today. "They've been looking into my 'past associations'," she says.'

'What does she mean?'

'You know what she means, what it always means. She says they're just checking to make sure there are no active Communists inside the school. She kept saying there's nothing to worry about.'

'So maybe there isn't.'

'Don't be naive. She kept waiting for me to deny I was a Communist. I wouldn't give her the satisfaction.'

'Don't look so surprised Sonia. Look what happened to those men on the *Daily News*. They've got all of us on lists, goodies and baddies. You just have to make one wrong move.'

'You're paranoid.' I don't want to hear her, her voice like the dread within me. Why when I have nothing to hide.

'We're just school teachers. What do we matter?'

'Don't you see? I've been found out. Don't you see now?'

Some of the teachers prepare for a month before open school week. Irene rehearsed every minute of her day with me. She would begin with math problems, one by one the good students trotting up to the front of the class to write their answers on the board. She was doing 'Our neighbors to the South' in Social Studies; she had gone over the questions many times so that students would know when to raise their hands and who would be called on. Each of them would stand, turn to face the parents at the back of the room, recite the crops of Colombia and Brazil while she held a pointer to a colored map. There was even a moment when her best student would walk ceremoniously to the pulpit she had set up next to her desk and recite 'The Road Not Taken'.

But I do not try so hard. I had the children make posters with the words 'Welcome Mothers' included in their design and these I arranged around the walls, choosing the best for the door, a picture by Susan Pritchard of three girls holding balloons with pictures of motherly faces inside. I make sure all the subjects are covered and that every child has a chance to say something, for even the shy ones want to speak on that day, and the slow ones know that for once they can raise their hands and not be declared wrong.

The mothers are supposed to arrive at nine when class begins but they drift in late. With each opening of the door, the children turn their heads and one of them blushes as he recognizes his mother who cannot resist waving before she tiptoes to the back with her head lowered and squeezes herself into one of the wooden chairs.

They are like giant moles driven out of their safe darkness, apologizing with their every movement for disturbing the teacher. What were they doing which always made them late? Did they stare out the window into the empty morning till they remembered that this day was different from all other days? They must listen to their children and know that other mothers would be listening too, that they might no longer be able to deny that their children were slow or noisy or only average. Perhaps this was why they stared at me not the children, that it was my hesitation, my dropping of the chalk that they noticed and kept in their minds when they came up afterwards to ask why the report card had said 'could do better'.

I look at the mothers ranged across the back of the room, most with their coats still on, their hands clasped on the desks like good children. Maybe it is their own failures they remember as they sit there.

I have not identified Christine's mother for the girl has avoided looking at the door. She looks relaxed for once, almost confident, for she knows no one will pick on her. Each of the children feels so singled out that they will not pinch her thin arms or knock her colored pencils to the floor. Even when she says something peculiar, they do not laugh for this will diminish all of them.

She is more alert than usual. She toils over a problem in long division which she would normally never attempt and when we do geography, her worst subject, she keeps raising her hand. But I never call on her for there are no half right answers in geography; I cannot disguise the girl's failures.

I ask her to read a stanza from a poem we are learning but she stumbles over the hard words and has to be helped. The mothers shift in their seats, cup their hands over their mouths. The children look embarrassed and begin to raise their hands in the hope that I will cut Christine short and call on one of them, but I make a gesture to them to lower their arms and let the girl continue till she reaches the end of the stanza and sits down, her face pale with exertion.

By midday the mothers rest their faces in their hands; one of them sleeps with her arms folded across her breasts. But the children do not notice. Their hands go up no matter what I say, the desperate flailing of those who have not yet scored a right answer or whose whispered correct guess was drowned out by another so eager that he did not wait to be called. And then there are the children who can never be sure they have done enough or that their mother will remember the smart thing they said early in the morning. Christine has given up trying. She doodles on her page with her head bowed, as if some great weight has fallen on her. Her mother's eyes.

But Christine's mother sees nothing of the morning. She arrives during assembly. A stylish woman, tall and lean with close-cropped black hair and a profile as sharp as the patent leather pocketbook she carries, she doesn't look like a mother. How could a dreamy child with a face out of a sepia photo have come from her?

'My daughter's got a belly ache,' she tells me. 'I better take her home.'

Christine often has a belly ache. She suffers from heartburn and nausea like an adult.

'Yes, of course. She didn't tell me.'

'She wouldn't. Not you. You're her favorite person.'

'Oh well. She's a very sweet girl.'

'You don't have to say that. She's going through a phrase. I know. I went through it. We all go through it and then we find out everyone else is crazy too.'

'She's got a lot of imagination.'

Christine's mother laughs at this. 'Some imagination. I knew who to expect. She draws pictures at home. Always the same picture of little match girl with frizzy hair just like her and guess who's the happy prince?' She touches my arm. 'Ever hear of a prince with shoulder-length curly brown hair? You're just like she drew you.'

91

She looks back at her daughter. 'Uh oh. I better go before she throws up right here.'

I turn to see the girl standing by the assembly door, her body curved over the pain in her belly.

13

Helen

The dream comes back to me when I'm in Social Studies and Mr. Cooperman is telling us about the Ku Klux Klan. We've just got through the Civil War and the Tea Pot Dome scandal. Everything has to have a moral with him; he doesn't just ask us to list the three causes of the war – cotton, slaves and industry – like we did in seventh grade. We have to think ourselves back to that time, pretend we're a runaway slave and then a Confederate soldier. We all think he's a hippy. Not that his hair is that long. It's the way he talks, so free with his words and never sitting at his desk but pacing back and forth and sometimes around the room like he has to go to the bathroom but decides to hold it all in.

The white hoods remind me. I was sitting before a mirror trying on my mother's hats, all of them on little stands like in the stores: a black crab with a veil, another made of soft grey felt with a brim at the front which dipped down like a creepy smile. But the one I stuck on my head was too large for me. It had a wide fur brim from which a soft white cone rose like the turban on a fairy tale sultan. It kept slipping down over my face, my neck ached from the weight of it.

I don't know why my feet were shaking when I woke up like I had had a nightmare. I knew in the dream that my mother wasn't around, that she had left the hats and would never come back. I don't understand. My mother doesn't wear hats like that except in the pictures when she was young. Nowadays she pulls a white wool cap over her hair in winter, pulls it right down over her ears and forehead so she looks like a man. 'Let's go already,' she says while I'm putting my hat on in front of the hall mirror, just like hers only with a pom pom. I remember now I used to have one when I was little with a peak and a pom pom which bobbed behind me as I walked so I felt like a queen. The boys called me 'witch' and tried to yank it off but my mother had tied it so tightly under my chin that all they could do was pull it down over my back.

With the black man she is hatless even though I can feel the cold, the tree behind them as bare as November. She cared what she looked like then, a hat would have squashed her curls. I haven't taken out the photographs since I came home late that night from Central Park. What am I afraid of? I think if my mother finds out she'll know everything about me.

But maybe I just don't care anymore; I've got other things on my mind. I'm meeting Sheila in the afternoons when she's not seeing Eddie. I joined the Boosters, a group of girls who sit on metal bleachers in the gym and shout cheers for the boys' basketball team. Most of the time when I come home, my mother is already there, standing before the window with her hands pressing down the metal slats of the venetian blinds so she can look at the street without being seen by the neighbors across the way. She never pulls up the blinds except on Sunday when my father lies around the house all day. I think she enjoys looking through them, they're bars on her cage, only she's the one protected.

When I was little I was always getting in her way. She was moving all the time, down on her knees in her bra and undies cleaning the toilet, rushing in and out of the building with bags of food, pulling off the tops of sour cream in the grocery to see if they were all right. Never could I find her still. But now she's in my way, following me into my room to ask why I left my clothes on the floor, pulling down my mini-skirt till she's stretched the material, picking up the extension by accident on purpose when I talk to Sheila. For once I know something she doesn't know. I can be silent like her. Pretend to be daydreaming when she asks me a question. I have secrets with Sheila to match the ones she used to whisper in my father's ear.

Even my uncle Leo notices the change in me. When we go over to my grandmother's for Passover he calls me 'young lady' which I hate because that's what Mr. Cotter, the dean in my junior high says when he's telling off some girl for wearing her skirt too short. 'Now young lady.' He wags his finger at her like she's not even trying to be fast but is just a stupid little girl.

We're all dressed up for the Seder though it's only in my grandmother's dinky little apartment. It's boring for me because my cousins are all grown-up; when my uncle Leo hides the afikomen, I'm the only one who looks. My cousin says all the blessings in Hebrew which I don't understand while my father acts like an idiot, wearing his yarmulkah lopsided, banging on his glass with a spoon and whining, 'When are we going to eat?' Just because he doesn't have a son who can bless the wine.

Once when I was little I saw the wine move in the glass when we let in Elijah, but now I smell the draft from the incinerator, the greasy cooking from the hallway which makes me want to puke. That's my job to open the door. My grandma used to keep it unlocked during the Seder but now we're all too afraid. Last year a black man with a knife pushed his way into an old woman's apartment on the floor below us. So it's him, not the prophet I'm looking out for when I open the door.

Afterwards the television comes on, my father sitting close to the screen with his sad clown's face, my cousins sprawled out on the sofa, my mother in the kitchen with her mother. My uncle chooses this moment to ask with a smile like he's blessing me, if I'm not sorry that I didn't have a religious education. Now that I'm a 'young lady' he can talk to me about these things. If my father hears he doesn't say anything. I say I don't know. My mother told me only stupid people believe in god. But why is she always raising her eyes to them, the jealous ones who don't want us to be happy?

Tomorrow we'll come back for the second Seder with my uncle Julius and aunt Norma. It's always been that way even before my grandfather died and left no will because he thought it was bad luck and my uncles started fighting over some old war bonds. But they can do no wrong. My mother scrubs out her mother's cabinets, takes her to Macy's to pick out a new house dress, argues with the social security office, but Leo and Julius come first with my grandmother because they're sons. Even my mother runs between them, always on the phone to one after she's talked to the other.

When we're out on the street my mother walks backward waiting for my grandmother to fling open the window and wave. That wave and the evening is over. My mother always says the same thing: 'It's really a Passover moon.' While my father and I rush through the chilly night to car, my mother continues to walk backward looking up at the sky with an expression which embarrasses me. We wait for her to get in; then just as my father gets the heat going, she rolls down the window. 'I'm hot,' she complains.

'She's got the flushes,' my father says.

'Cut it out,' my mother says, but she's back to her old self.

The dream comes again on Seder night, the table with the funny hats and me alone in my mother's chair looking in the mirror, the big clumsy hat with the white cone sagging on my head. Only I can't see my face. I keep looking in the mirror as if my lost face is somewhere inside the glass. I move closer and closer to the mirror but it grows dark and still I cannot find myself. The hat grows softer and longer till the fur brim falls over my eyes and mouth and I can taste the dead fox. I'm tumbling out of my chair, falling down some fire escape till I reach bottom with a jump on my bed.

14

Sonia

Nightfall, The Museum V

So we love
awkwardly
struggling for dominion amid stone shadows

I run all the way from the subway and now as I cross the great oblongs of light thrown across the floor by the tall windows, I think I might not be able to speak. So silent in here. I am glad Caleb does not look up as I approach. Just as I reach his desk the door of the library is flung open and I hear the sound of children's voices, the shush shushing of a teacher and imagine for a moment that my own class has followed me in here. But it is a kindergarten of Negroes with a white teacher. They begin to run each with a partner and the teacher rushes ahead with her arm raised.

Caleb is roused from his work by their voices and looks up with a grin as the children pass his desk. When he notices me, his face grows puzzled then stern. He always said he had several lives and liked to keep them all separate.

'What are you doing here? Aren't you supposed to be at school?'

'I am but...'

He looks me over. 'So what is it? Anything wrong?'

'Can we go somewhere?'

He glances at his watch. 'I'll have to take an early lunch. That's if I can find someone to cover for me.' Then he leans across the desk and whispers, 'What are you coming in here for looking like a crazy woman?'

'I gotta talk to you. Please. I can't wait. I came all the way down on my lunch hour.'

'Stay here.' He walks over to the woman at the counter who nods her head, then looks over at me.

I hear the faint sounds of the teacher reading to her class, the question she asks and the answers the children give in unison always with one high voice trailing behind the others.

Caleb beckons to me from the counter and I follow him out of the library, running to keep up with him on the bright street.

'It's my mother,' I say.

He turns and starts to put his arm around me. 'Oh,' he says, 'I'm sorry.'

'No not that. They told her about you. My brothers. I told them not to tell, it would upset her. When they threatened I didn't believe them. Why should they do such a thing?'

'You mean to tell me all this time you've been keeping it from them?'

'I couldn't tell them. You know I couldn't.'

'What are you, ashamed?'

'You know that's not it. I just couldn't tell them.'

'I don't believe it. All this time.'

'But I couldn't tell them.'

My voice is a whine.

'And then my father, if he found out he'd have another stroke.'

'I thought. Well, forget what I thought.'

I had hoped to be enfolded by him, that after the harsh voice of my mother on the phone I could run to him and be taken in. But he turns from me, turns and turns again; I keep shifting my position on the sidewalk to keep in front of him.

'You've got to understand.'

'What's there to understand? You're still a little girl. Daddy's little girl. Only now you've gone too far.'

I take his hand. He does not pull away but his hand is limp in my palm.

'My mother said I killed my father. He's sick with knowing.' I do not tell him that mom said I was unclean now.

Caleb's face softens. 'You should have told them earlier.'

'What difference would it have made?'

'It wouldn't have been such a shock. They could know about me gradually.'

'How can something like that be gradual?'

'So what are you going to do?'

Why had I thought he would take care of me? He pulls his hand from mine, folds his arms in front of his chest.

'I don't know. What do you think?'

He shrugs. 'I don't know what to tell you.'

'But you must help me.'

'Look I don't want any trouble.'

The sunlight burns my eyes, my throat.

'Maybe there's no future in it,' he says, 'If I go away, you'll get back together with your folks. Your father will forgive and forget. You'll meet someone else. Some Jewboy. You'll marry and be just like your mother wants. You may never be happy but who is? What do you think? Cut it off short and sweet?'

I cannot speak. I am swollen inside from holding back. He says, 'Anyway how can I help you? I'm the problem see?'

I put out my hands like a child learning to walk but he pushes them down. A sound comes out of me. He puts his hands on my shoulders; when I look up at him, half blind with tears, his face is like some idol.

'Don't get so dramatic woman. I was just giving you an out. You gotta talk to them. Your brothers full of vitriol. Maybe if you talk to your daddy yourself, eh.'

I shake my head. My mother said I couldn't come home now I had dirtied myself with some *shvartzeh*.

'Yeah. You go there tonight and I'll call you maybe over the weekend.'

Again my hands reach out to him and he holds me for a moment. 'Now, do you think you can go back to school? Because I gotta get back. You caught me at a bad moment.'

I arrive back just in time to lead my class from the schoolyard, where they line up after lunch, back to the classroom. They resist, wanting to remain outside in the sunlight smelling of soil and sweet fumes; my voice is faint as I urge them in. I am glad to get away from the brilliance, to meet the gloomy corridors of the school. In the classroom I stand in the shafts of light waiting for the clamor to die down, but the children are hot and restless from playing in the sun and cannot settle. I have not the strength give them the lesson I planned about atoms.

'What do you think is the smallest thing?' I would say and wait for their wrong answers: a bug crawling on the kitchen floor, a red ant who lives where the retards dug the soil in the far corner of the school yard, the dust in the arc of light above my desk. 'What are we made of, all of us?' Instead I hear myself tell them in a dull voice to take out a sheet of paper and a pencil. They groan for this usually means a test. They are to write a composition taking up one side of the paper about the coming of spring.

But they are not fooled and soon Linda catches Sam's eye and begins an exaggerated twiddle of her thumbs. Jeffrey starts to play the drums on his desk.

'Have you written your composition?' I yell out. Jeffrey holds up a piece of paper with the writing in a loose scrawl down the page.

'Then if you've finished, put your head down on the desk.'

This is baby stuff. Jeffrey drops his chin on his palm and pretends to snore. Something is going around the back of the room, I see the shifting of heads, sly faces, but I wait. If I try to intercept the message I might fail, I might never discover the piece of paper deep in their fists, their pockets, the password fallen from their lips, buried in the darkness beyond their eyes.

Christine writes slowly with her face close to the page. I watch her for a moment as if gathering strength from this picture of quiet diligence, then walk round to the back of the room where the commotion like a slow wave is moving from desk to desk. When they see me coming, they lower their faces, hands pressed against their mouths to keep the laughter in. I hear the tearing of paper, a yelp from the front of the room and turn to see Linda run to her seat. Christine is rocking, her cries like an angry bird.

Why is it always Linda the class choose for their dirty work? A chubby girl with smooth Cleopatra hair, a shiny face and fixed smile like a rubber doll. 'Fatso,' they call her in the yard when she runs round the bases during punchball. I yank Linda from her seat and drag her to the front of the room. I am holding her arm so tightly that the girl begins to cry.

'Shush Christine.' But the girl cannot stop her rocking and moaning, will not uncurl her fists for Linda has torn the page she worked over like parchment. I let go of Linda and ease Christine out of her seat. Then I call up to the front Michael Schiffer and Pauline Gardino, the class president and vice president, and tell them to take charge which means they can write down the names of anyone who talks or even stirs from their seat. It is a rare chance to exercise the office they hold for only a month. They know that if there are no names on the board, if the class can be heard from the hallway I will tell them they have not done their job. They stand proudly in front of their classmates, the president holding the wooden pass which is the symbol of their shaky power. Only one child can leave the classroom at a time, and he has to raise his hand and beg for the pass from them.

'I'm relying on you.' What I always say though I don't need to. Once they leave their desks, once they stand where I normally do, they turn against the other children and become more harsh than I will ever be.

I take the two girls out into the dim hallway and make them face each other. I pull Linda's arm forward, grab hold of the wrist and flap the hand in front of Christine who puts her hands out in front of her face, shuts her eyes as if the blow has come.

'Here,' I say, 'Here. You want to hit her?' Linda tries to pull back her arm but I hold her.

'Is that what you what?'

Linda shakes her head and lets the tears flow down her doll face. She is an easy crier and does not even wipe her nose. I imagine her in the bath, the shiny arms rising above the bubbles, her mother perched on the tub cooing: 'How's my baby doll?'

I wait for Linda to stop crying, then begin to lead them both back to the classroom. But Christine will not move. A sour smell rises from her body rigid with anger and fear; the cold hard fist I grasp does not feel like flesh.

'Go back,' I tell Linda who stares at Christine. 'I want to see a page of writing from you.'

When Linda leaves Christine seems to come back to life. She screams and chokes like a colicky baby. I drag her to the teachers' room, dark and empty, the imprint of women's bodies still on the yellow vinyl sofa. I sit her down and go to the sink in the corner to pour her a glass of water.

The screams grow louder. She has begun rocking again. 'Stop it Christine.' I stand in front of her. 'You must stop it. You'll make yourself sick.' The girl is possessed. What can I do, slap her back to normal like in the movies? 'She'll cry it out,' my mother used to say when her grandchildren threw tantrums, only Christine's eyes are dry.

'Here. Drink some water.' I hold out the glass but she does not seem to notice. I sit down next to her and put my arm around her shoulders, but she continues to rock as if the paper Linda had torn had been her body and she could not mend. I pull the girl close, her frail body still so cold that I shiver from the contact. I hug her to bring back the warmth. We are alone on the tundra, my body keeping a tiny child alive. Christine quiets down and as we sit with our eyes shut, I feel the girl hug me back, the light from her filigree body grows till it envelops us, till my heart sluggish from the cold begins to beat with the child's fierce pulse and we sit in a yolk of sun above the frozen land.

My mother follows me about the house. Her sharp words over the phone meant nothing, were curses she could not control and now she flutters around me, her big girl, her cuckoo.

'You're not going to get serious with him, are you?'

'Leave me alone, will you?'

'How can I? Look what happens to you. Tell me the truth. You're not really serious?'

'What do you want me to say? He's my boyfriend.' The first time I actually talked about Caleb as if he were an ordinary man.

My mother cannot sit still. She follows me into the kitchen, tugs at my sleeve when I ignore her.

'What do you mean by that?' She pulls at my chin. 'Look at me.

You want to marry a *shvartzeh*? You want to have colored babies nobody will want?' Then conscious of the nearness of the hall door, of the neighbors who will lick their fat lips over her daughter's fall, she begins to whisper: 'What are you, crazy? You must be crazy. Julius said he's an older man too.'

When I entered the dirt brown building, the heavy doors closing behind me like stones, the smell of sour grease and cabbage; when Mom drew back the door to the apartment, such a small woman to pull the weight of it, I wondered why I had been afraid to come home. Everything was as it had always been, would never change even if I did. I felt a great weariness settle on me; if I lay down in the back room and let sleep possess me I would wake in the darkness of early evening as if nothing had happened to me.

'Look. It's none of your business.' I pour my coffee, pick up the cup with both hands.

My mother forgets for a moment that she is ready to disinherit her daughter. 'You want a Danish? It's fresh.' She pulls open a white wax bag and puts it under my nose.

'But there's only one left.'

'Finish it. I bought it for your father but he's lost his appetite.'

I bring my Danish and coffee out to the table in the foyer. Mom follows with a plate. 'Here. You'll make crumbs.'

'Where's Pop?'

'He's sleeping. He hasn't said anything since we found out. He's in a state of shock. I can take it better than him. I get upset but I can cope. Not him. What you did to him.' She shakes her head. 'When Leo told us, he just went into the bedroom and lay down.'

She looks down at me almost puzzled. How had she produced this great sulking girl? Her fingers curl around the edge of the table; she wants her needles but to knit now would be to show acceptance of what I have done. I know she does not really believe I make love with a colored man. Not our Sonia. Our Sonia will not let anyone go into her.

'Where are you going?' For I have brought the coffeecup and dish into the kitchen and am running the hot water.

'Home. Where do you think?'

'But you just got here.'

I put my jacket on; I came to see Pop but now I do not care. But as I turn towards the door, we hear the whispering of my father's slippers. He looks small from where I stand, a balding old man in a bathrobe, dragging his slippers along the corridor he travels down everyday.

I think he could not have known I was there for he never appears in his night clothes when I visit. I come forward for his kiss like a benediction. Hadn't Mom kissed me hello despite what she said? But he turns away from me and goes to sit in his usual place in the living room, adjusts his robe over his knees with his good hand, then gets up again to switch on the television.

'Pop, you're not mad?' I cross the livingroom with my mother behind me.

He looks away from me at the screen, his profile pale and hard in the light thrown by the television.

'See. See what you've done to him,' my mother says.

His hand suddenly reaches out to me. I have been bad Papa but can't we be friends again? He does not take the hand I extend; he grabs my shoulder, all his strength in the hand which squeezes my flesh, the hand which once molded iron from the flames.

'Pop you're hurting me.' I try to shake off his hand, then peel the fingers from my shoulder. I twist in his hand while he stares at me. He pulls me forward. I can see his mouth working, the words are there already but his mouth needs time to shape them. Then he whispers a word out of the corner of his lips as if he is passing a secret.

'What is it?'

He draws closer and speaks into my ear, though now his voice is loud enough to hear.

'Lilith,' he says.

I feel only the cessation of pain when he lets go of my shoulder. I do not understand.

'What do you mean?'

'Lilith,' he repeats and puts his hand on my head.

He is blessing me like the old men in my child's book of bible stories. Even as he pushes my head away I remember Isaac and Abraham, the hand of God averting the sacrifice.

15

Helen

'He breathes like an animal,' Sheila says. I can see it's not enough to have Eddie on top of her: she has to tell me how once she fainted while he was frenching her, how she woke not knowing what he had done. I take the stories home with me and think about them while I rub against the gold throw pillows on the couch. But it's not Eddie touching her, skinny, sharp Eddie with looks like lightening rods but someone whose face I can't see. Sometimes a dark husky man with a woolen cap.

I think about getting my mother to talk about the photographs, but her face is so hard in the morning bedroom light. She marches past my bed as if I'm not there, pulls up the blinds and begins dusting. What if I said, 'Ma, I saw you with a black man.' Then she would turn, her face would change like the face in my dream, my mirror face disappearing, then appearing when I'm not looking. She'd become the woman she is in the photograph. I don't know why I'm scared when I think of her talking about it like she and that man really happened. Part of me is hoping she'll say he was just some friend of a friend and then we can be the way we were before.

Sometimes she turns to me, stares into my face before speaking and I think now she's going to tell me. My heart starts pounding, I try to think of something to say to stop her but she never says anything. So why do I feel it's on the tip of her tongue, why do I drop hints so she'll say, she'll reveal herself like a robber, a murderer coming back to the scene of his crime?

When I tell her Sheila's dating a black boy, she asks, 'Does her mother know?'

'I don't know. I guess so. Sheila does whatever she wants. Nobody can tell her anything.'

'Like you,' she says.

I ignore this. 'Sheila says black boys are more mature.'

My mother snorts at this but I go on glad to see I'm getting something out of her. 'She said even if she breaks up with him she's not going back to white boys, no way.'

'She sounds like a jerk. Don't you have any other friends? You pick them.'

'What's wrong with her? You're just prejudiced.' I'm watching her face but she doesn't even blush.

'She's not your type. She sounds wild.' Then she looks at me like she knows what I'm thinking. I hate that look, like I've got no secrets.

'Your father would be very upset if you ever.' She can't even say it like she's afraid if she says it, it'll happen. She turns her back, scoops up the covers on the bed I've just left, the dust flying in the sun around her.

I want to ask 'what about you?' but I've gone too far already and from the back she looks like the battle-ax my father's always calling her.

She begins shaking each cover out the window. Once she lost a pair of my pajamas that way. It was caught up in a blanket and fell seven flights before landing in a tree. She had to ask a policeman to get it down. Whenever she makes mistakes like blowing the fuse or leaving the keys in the door, which she does often considering how perfect she's always pretending to be, she always blames one of us. 'You make me addle-brained,' she'll say, 'you make me crazy.'

She pulls in the blanket and begins folding, then looks up at me. 'What are you gawking at? I thought you were meeting your friend.'

But I see she's not mad at me but someone else. I feel satisfied as I walk away but I don't know why.

Sheila shouts to me in the hall as we pass that she has to see me after school. When I hesitate she stares at me with her big fish eyes. Her chubby cheeks look all pink and wrinkled like she's been sleeping with her face squashed against the pillow. So I know that for once she wants me more than I want her. I feel good strolling away down the hall waving at girls I know.

We walk across to the reservoir. I haven't been back since we saw the man. When she suggested it I wanted to say no but she wasn't in the mood to give in. I knew if I kept on she'd make fun of me.

Eddie wants to break up with her. She can tell because she went to his party and when she walked in the door he just waved to her but didn't come over. Just like that he cooled. He was with his black girlfriend but then she always featured. He had his white and black girlfriends, one for each side of the cake he said. Everyone knew he was dropping her because his friends started coming onto her like they thought she was easy.

'I can't understand it. We were so tight. Friday night I was lying on his chest, he told me he loved me.'

I have never seen her hurt before. Always the boys she went out with were a joke. I realize I don't want her to break with Eddie; it's as if I'm losing something too even though he scares me.

I say, 'Maybe he was just in a bad mood.'

'Nah.'

'I bet that's what it was. He'll call.'

'Don't be so stupid.'

'What are you getting mad at me for?'

She doesn't say anything. Suddenly she gets up from the bench and begins walking around the edge of the reservoir. I sit there even though I'm afraid to be alone after what happened. I watch her disappear around the bend, then come back again, walking towards me with her hand beckoning. I shrug my shoulders. I'm thinking it's her own fault for being so easy with him. My mother would say he was just using her, her favorite expression. When I was little if she didn't like a friend, she'd say they didn't really care for me, they were using me. Using me for what? She'd say I was a fool for asking.

When she comes closer I can see she's been crying. 'Don't you want to walk around?' she asks.

I get up slowly like I'm doing her a favor. She takes my arm as if she needs me to brace herself. I'm pleased inside though I try not to smile. But after we walk some time I feel the weight of her on me and I want her the same as before.

'They'll think we're lessies,' I say.

'Let them.'

If only everything could be put back the way it was. I try to think of some way he could be with her again. I don't say anything because I know she'll get mad at me for raising her hopes.

All the way home on the bus I can't sit still. Something I depended on is gone. Like losing my mother in the dream where she's on the other side of a road walking fast and I can't reach her. Never can I get across that road.

I know I have to see the photographs again even if it means canceling with Sheila so I can be home when my mother is not. But it turns out not so easy. My father gets the grippe, coughing and bringing up phlegm for a week in the bedroom. My mother spends her time shaking a thermometer and making him tea in one of her blue fiesta bowls because he never likes it too hot. You can sink into her when you're sick, even her touch is different. She looks at you like she's trying to figure out a problem in your face.

So I have to wait till the room is free again and the waiting makes me nervous, makes me want the photographs too much. I'm irritable with my father even though he's sick. My mother watches, takes me aside to ask if I've got my period.

'Leave me alone.' I push her hand off my shoulder.

'Who's touching you? Who could ever touch you?' But she looks sad.

When the blue felt purse isn't there in the cool folds of her sweater, I start to rummage through the drawer. I feel sick and my hands begin lifting her sweaters and not caring how they fall back into a jumble and she would know someone had been through her clothes. I try the other drawers but can't find the purse I stitched for her so long ago. I'm crying and cursing her for hiding the photographs from me, for why else would she move the purse? So I would think maybe I'd never seen her black man. She has taken him away from me just like she pulled a silver Christmas tree ball from my mouth when I was little and wanted what the Gentiles had, just like she pulled my hands from between my legs. This is not mine, didn't I know? Nothing is mine that was not hers first.

16

Sonia

Nightfall, The Museum VI

Before morning
before the lone watchman paces the room
I return him to his pedestal
no god has intervened on my behalf
his seed cannot bring forth children of the earthly sort.

Everything in a shroud. The landing with the light still broken, the kitchen, my bedroom, all silent and cold, without shadows, the air still heavy from Irene's cooking.

Go out and come in again. Go out and come in again. Who had always said that?

I hear the shuffle of slippers from behind Irene's curtain. As I switch on the kitchen light, she emerges in her bathrobe.

'Where you been?'

She never asked before, our comings and goings make no difference to each other.

'Home. You're sleeping already?'

Irene sits down at the table. She wants to talk. I remain standing. I want only to lie in the darkness of my room, to draw the covers over me and know that no light can reach me.

'I was trying to.'

'I woke you then. I'm sorry.'

'Caleb called. To see how you were.'

'Oh maybe I better call him.'

Irene puts up her hand. How small she looks, expectant like a child full of answers.

'Harvey was over. You won't believe this. He proposed.'

I cannot concentrate on what Irene is saying; I must call him, must must.

'Are you with me? I said he wants to marry me.'

'That's nice. I mean.'

'I told him I'd think about it. He didn't like that. He said if I loved him I'd know right off the bat.'

'So do you?'

'Was it your mother or mine who said "You don't have to love them"? Anyway it's not that. He's not what I imagined for myself. A salesman. He's such a mediocrity.'

I try to listen but think of Caleb turning his face from me. If I do not call now.

'But if you love him.'

'What does that mean anyway? That you enjoy going to bed with someone, that's all.'

'Irene. C'mon.'

'So you're in love with Caleb.' Her face is sly.

'Do me a favor. Don't bring me into this.'

'You are aren't you? Well good luck to you.'

She stares at me but I don't give her any satisfaction.

'Harvey says if we're not going to marry we should stop seeing each other.'

'It's just a threat.'

'I don't think so. Harvey wants to have a home to come back to. If it's not me, he'll find someone else. Can you see me a housewife to him? I mean he's not very smart is he? I thought when the time came I'd find someone different. More my level.'

I sit down with her. What if Irene leaves to get married? I cannot afford the rent alone, and there is no one I can ask to move in with me. I cannot go home now not even for a short time unless I give up Caleb. And even then I will have to beg forgiveness.

'I thought you didn't care about getting married.'

'How can I not care? Sonia, sometimes I think you've got tunnel vision. You can't see to the left or right of your nose.'

I have no fight in left me, my voice a tired whine which so irritates Irene. 'You told me once you never wanted to be like the teachers at the school.'

'That's different. They were born to be hausfraus.'

'So you're going to say no.'

'If I do, I'll be high and dry. There goes my pathetic social life, and then if I lose my job.'

'You won't. She just asked you some questions, that's all.'

'That's enough. As soon as they start poking around your past you're finished. Some of the people who lost their jobs weren't even members. They were just named by somebody and then they were fired. Just like that. Off with your head.'

'But not schoolteachers. Who cares about us?'

'They do. Even if you denounce your past. Even then. When I joined the party, I was only a kid, what did I know? We were all friends. We sang together. If someone had a sandwich they broke it in as many pieces as they could and shared it.'

'You were a party member? I didn't know you actually joined.'

'Don't sound so shocked. I was only in a couple of years. I got bored. People were getting up and saying the same things and nothing was happening. Nobody knew we existed, the police didn't even bother breaking up our demonstrations. And nobody really cared about anyone else when it came down to it. Your comrade could steal your boyfriend and if you said anything they'd just say you were possessive. You loved like a capitalist. So I left. I probably was in it for less than two years. But that's enough for them. They're just looking for someone they can pull out of line.'

'But even if God forbid you lost your job, you can't marry him just for security.'

'Why not? So he's crude and we have nothing to talk about outside of bed. He'll be a good provider won't he?'

I shake my head.

'Plenty of women would. Don't be so naive. That's the way our mothers married. I'm just a fool. My mother keeps saying "You're not getting any younger."'

'Since when did you care what your mother says?'

'I don't. I'm just saying.' She looks tired, beaten. 'Why don't you sit down, you're making me nervous. You can call Caleb later.'

Past midnight and his voice is thick with sleep. 'That bad?' he mumbles when I tell him about my father. 'Well we'll have to see. Tomorrow maybe I'll call you.'

I am shivering when I get off the phone. If Irene leaves me I will be like the woman my father named, with only shame to clothe my naked body.

I push against the thick green waters, my legs flowing out behind me, the shore stretching flat and pink to the blackened museum. When I reach the island, I see it crumbling, doors open, cases broken and pillaged, statues torn from their pedestals. Sunlight through the high windows bleaches the black mummies. I am swimming through the empty rooms to the exit, the noise from the wide street bursting over me, my body still slimy from the sea. They rush past me down the wide avenue, a crowd pressing against the horizon. I turn to go back but the guard has opened the door to the museum and people flow through the vestibule. I was always alone but now everyone will know and pity me. I cover my body with my hands.

❄ ❄ ❄

'Irene might be getting married,' I tell Caleb.

'Not her. Who'd propose to her?'

'Don't be so cruel. Harvey wants to settle down.'

'Doesn't mean she does. She strikes me as the spinster type.'

'She's thinking it over.'

'So where does that leave you? You better start looking around for a new roommate.'

If he said 'marry me', what would I do? If only there was a way we could be together but nobody to know.

'I guess so.'

He draws me towards him on the bed. 'Because you can't afford that dump on your own.'

'Maybe I'll move to a smaller place. An efficiency.'

'Yeah. You don't need her.' He pulls my hair back hard and rises above me. When he tries to pull out, I hold on to him. Why does he always waste himself?

'Jesus Christ, are you crazy? You want a black baby eh?' He pushes me off the bed. 'Quick go wash yourself.'

When I return I say, 'I want you not to pull away like that, it hurts me.'

But he is silent. He lies beside me, his arms under his head, his eyes shut. I think he has a poem coming on. The muse is no lady he's always saying, she'll come along when you've just emptied yourself.

Caleb waits for me at the top of the dazzling white stairs, his face in the sun's shadow; a dark heavy god, he waits while I climb, shielding my eyes from the glare of the stone steps. I take his arm and we walk into the great high hall of the museum, then into the Greek and Roman rooms.

He says, 'It's easier if we separate.'

I wander off to look at the broken bowls, the oil lamps, the amulets. I will myself not to look at him but after a few minutes I turn. He is watching the guard and when the man steps into the other room he puts his hand on the ass of a statue of Apollo.

I am standing before Greek vases when I realize I am alone in the room with only the guard's eyes upon me. I try to take my time, moving in slow motion like the men and women dancing, bringing water, making sacrifices on the black and sienna vases. But as I walk from one glass case to another, the figures began to run, their arms and legs a tangle of movement around the vases, round and round. I flee from them but Caleb is not in the next room, not in the dark corridor. I run through the remaining rooms, then out to the vestibule where a couple with their little girl gape at me as they wait for the elevator.

He has gone back to the first room we entered together, to an archaic statue of Zeus. He looks up at me when I rush in the room, then back to the broken stone face.

'Hey. Calm down.' He puts out a hand as if afraid I might shatter the face still further. 'What's wrong with you?' Because I am panting. 'Someone chasing you?' He grasps my shoulder hard.

'I thought I lost you.'

114

'Like being with a child.' He cups his hand under my chin. I shake free. 'So what do you say we get a bite to eat?'

Like an underground palace this grand room of mirrors where skinny green gargoyles and stained cherubs spit water in a marble pool. When I used to peek into the museum's fancy restaurant, Julius would say what you want to go in there for, you get the same food for less downstairs.

Caleb tells me about a new poem he's working on, how he can turn it around in his head in the mornings at the library when no one comes by to ask him foolish questions. Like nothing he's ever done before, an epic, only contemporary with characters from Harlem and a refrain he lifted from some calypso music. No one will like his hero, least of all white people, but he is tired of worrying what they'd think.

I rub a drop of coffee into the black marble table.

He has never been so expansive, talking about his poetry before it is even born, talking about white people like I'm not one.

'He's a preacher but he hates the Christian god.'

His father was a religious man with a temper Caleb proudly claimed as his inheritance.

'Because the Christian god brought slavery. He's the god for whites only.'

'So your poem is all about how bad we are.'

'I don't think of you as white. No Jew is, not really.'

I ignore this. 'What about the other characters? Are they based on people you know?'

'You could say.' He winks at me. 'Don't worry, you're not in it.'

Someday I will show him my poems, the pieces of dreams I write in my black and white notebook. They are all about me, I know no other characters.

'That wasn't what I meant. I never even thought.'

'Don't be so touchy.'

He does not see what I am driving at, has turned my question against me.

'You're not touchy?'

'Not like you. Compared to you I got skin tough as a bison.'

'How would you feel?' I press my eyes shut.

'Hey. Don't get so upset.'

'How would you feel if your parents practically disowned you? My father called me Lilith. I don't even know what he meant.'

'Lilith was an evil woman. The first bitch.' He looks at me with a sly smile.

'It's not funny. It felt like he was cursing me.'

'What do you want me to say? You keep telling me about your parents. I've never met them and they're against me. Why should I feel guilty?'

'I didn't say you should.'

'But that's how you make me feel.'

'I'm not trying to make you feel any way. But you're involved. You're the reason.'

'Christ, how do you think that makes me feel? I don't want to hear about it anymore. Your daddy's prejudiced. That's all.'

I reach for his hand. He allows me to hold it, to turn his palm upward and trace the thin white rivers. He leans back in the chair, his face drawn away from me.

'What are they afraid of? That I'm going to marry you? I'm not marrying anyone, you can tell them. I've been through it. Tell them. They'll be relieved.'

I drop his hand. It is as if he has shattered some invisible glass which enclosed us but which we hadn't noticed till it crashed about our bodies.

'I'm tired of it. Daddy's little girl. Still under his thumb. My daughter keeps asking why can't I see you on Saturdays anymore? What can I say, that I have a white girlfriend who's too bigoted to meet you?'

He never said anything before about his daughter. I thought he wanted to keep me away from the girl, that he was as ashamed as me.

'That's not true. I just feel uncomfortable.'

'Why?'

'I don't know. Maybe because we're not married.'

He raises his eyes. 'C'mon Sonia. You just don't want to face it.

116

It's all right, one colored man. Maybe. Maybe if you shut your eyes while we're making love, maybe I'm not even colored. But if I have a daughter, a colored daughter.'

I want to say that I cannot not bear for him to have this daughter, that it is impossible the two of us should appear before him, that if the daughter is there I cannot exist.

'You know something, I wish you were Lilith.'

I stand up. He reaches across the table and grabs my arm.

'Get down woman. You're not pulling that one on me.' We struggle but I cannot break free of him. I sit down again, but turn my face from him.

I stare at the water which rises from the mouth of the green sprite who is neither male nor female. I tilt my head so the sound comes clearer than the deep voice of the man opposite me.

'You hear?' He shakes my arm.

When I turn towards him, it is as if I have come a great distance. An old Negro man sits there with weary eyes and worn brown skin, a beard beginning to show white. I think, 'What am I doing with him?'

17

Helen

I keep looking for the photographs, searching the same place because maybe she'll put them back. Sometimes I think she knows I know and smiles because once again she's got something I want. Now that I can't see them I could beg from her like in the old days. When I asked enough times a story would drop from her lips, always the same story to warn me, about the little girl who left her friends to go off with a strange man who gave her poisoned candy cane. Just as she was about to lick it her mother came running around the block.

'How did she know the candy cane was poisoned?' I'd ask.

'Because she knew about the man. She told her daughter not to go with strangers but she wouldn't listen until it was almost too late.'

My father's suddenly after me to go to some day camp this summer. My mother's been talking I know and he doesn't want me hanging around with Sheila, meeting black boys in the park, seeing dirty movies on hot Saturdays. I don't tell them Eddie's broken up with Sheila and now she's not seeing anyone. My father's petrified I'll end up like her; I can tell because he keeps shoving his ape face at me every time I say I'm not doing anything as babyish as day camp.

'What do you mean you don't want to go? You're anti-social, that's the trouble with you.'

They take you somewhere everyday on the bus, to Jones Beach, Rye or the pool and there's even an overnight trip in some camp in Bear Mountain. I thought I was finished with camps. When I was little we went to bungalow colonies where I was pushed into day camp with a lot of girls who all knew each other from previous summers. It was like school. If you didn't find a friend right away you were stuck making lanyards with the counselor.

Parents always think you want to be with kids all the time, the more, the better. So they put you at children's tables at hotels; at Bar Mitzvahs you get stuck with creepy little boys who've all been to Hebrew school together.

'Go with them,' my mother said when I was too scared to go into the kindergarten.

I started walking into the classroom past another girl who was crying with her face to the wall. When I turned around my mother was gone.

They say it's not that they want to get rid of me. Just they figure you feel so at home with your own kind, the last thing you'd want is to be with them.

When we came home after a week at Green Acres, I heard my father tell his friend over the phone, 'I can recommend it. Helen had the time of her life. She went right to the teen table and that was the last we saw of her.' He sounded proud and I don't know why because all I did was trail around behind two other girls who were chasing a waiter. One of them kept throwing a *Bride Magazine* at him. When I ran up to my parents while they were sitting by the pool, my father said, 'Where's your friends? You lost them?' Then he laughed to one of the other men.

My mother said nothing; she let me sit on the arm of her wooden lounge chair while she read. She always has a grumpy look when we go to one of these places and I knew she wouldn't mind if I stayed with her awhile. It meant she didn't have to try to talk to any of the women. 'Those women,' she called them as if they were made of different flesh from her. When one of them asked her to play cards with them, she would say, 'we're just going in together'. She'd reach out to me. 'Quick, quick.' Her mouth shaped the words. I would pull her up from the depths of the chair. While I was still getting into prayer position for my dive, she jumped into the pool, swam underwater for as long as she could, then came up suddenly like an astronaut in her slick white cap.

We never went to the same place twice even if my father liked it, because my mother always wrinkled up her nose: 'When I think back,' she'd say, 'well it was a dive, wasn't it?' He'd argue with her, his face all jowls, his hang-dog look my mother calls it. But once she called a place a dive it was tainted and we could never go back.

We stopped going to bungalow colonies during August. 'A month is too long,' my mother said, 'to be in the country.' Now it's crummy hotels for two weeks. 'Rustic,' they called themselves. Deer Park Farm, The Pines, Hilltop Haven where we stayed in a little white wooden cabin with a heart above the front door, had hot dogs and baked beans in the main house and swam in the mud hole they called a lake. After my father moved to a bigger store we went to ritzier places named after the owners – The Goldbergs, The Steins, Tauber's – with shows on Saturday nights, masquerade parties, a golf course and Olympic swimming pool and rooms like real hotels with wall to wall carpets and a fan which came on with the light in the bathroom.

But they were all dives to my mother. Always the same hairy men played cards by the pool, while the women lay like mummies in the sun, their tanned faces like shrunken heads, their bare brown necks and wrists hung with heavy gold jewelry. Sometimes we met my father's friends and my mother had to socialize with their wives. My mother has no friends, just the women she passes on the stoop and nudges her cart against in the supermarket. 'They're not my type,' she's always saying. But who is?

They're nagging me so much I give in. I'll go for a month and see how I like it. I figure I can still see Sheila on the weekends. It's the photographs I'm worried about because by the time I get home from camp everyone will be around. But I can't let them go, now that she's hid them from me.

The bus picks us up under the overhead subway out on Pelham Parkway. I have my beach bag with my striped bikini I got in Alexander's, my towel, my tunafish sandwich and a bottle of Coppertone. It reminds me of school, the girls who know each other bunched up at the back with their bags tipped over their shoulders, the others in a straggly line, too afraid to talk to those beside them, wondering who they'll sit next to.

I notice a couple of my so-called friends from the popular clique at school standing with the girls at the back, but they don't beckon to me. Since I've become Sheila's friend again, they've dropped me like a hot cake. My mother's expression.

When I get on the bus I'll just go for the first empty seat and hope someone, not a creep, sits next to me. Because that's how it begins, the wrong person next to you or the seat empty and you trying to pretend that it's all right, you're happy looking out the window. Or sitting on the aisle poking your head out to see all the action at the back, laughing like you're in on it. But knowing after days pass that no one else will go near you, except the others who sit alone. I've seen it happen.

The girls who know each other all head for the back of the bus, so do the clowns, the boys tense with trying to drag a laugh out of them. The others just wander on, the short chubby boys who look like they're still in Hebrew school, the left over girls with their bags dangling from their pale arms, the one black girl who cranes her neck to see who is sitting where before choosing the front seat. What is she looking for? One of her own?

The counselor comes on, begins reading out the names, then takes off her glasses and introduces herself as Gloria. I think she's old for a counselor. In the bungalow colonies they were teenagers or college girls. Gloria doesn't even wear shorts like the rest of us. She's all dressed up in white culottes, a knitted turquoise shell and two long strands of pearls, 'fakes' she tells us later. She's tall with long flat freckled arms. What I can see of her face is glazed with pancake makeup. Through the sweat of the other kids, I get a whiff of her. She smells like a beauty parlor. Somehow I feel better for I know she can never make friends with the kids at the back already giggling while she speaks. She acts like she doesn't notice, turns to sit down with the black girl.

Gloria is a schoolteacher. She tells us everything about herself, how she's divorced and dating a shrink, the cute little efficiency she lives in, the Chinese food she can't live without. Wherever we go she finds herself a deck chair and begins spreading coconut oil over her body. I never see her go into the water.

I find it doesn't matter who I sit next to because everyone not with the group at the back is out of it. We're all creeps together.

The first day I'm stuck with a serious pudgy girl who brings out a Macy's bag filled with photographs of The Rolling Stones, a WRKO tee-shirt she'd won by phoning in the correct date of birth of John Lennon and millions of buttons with stupid sayings like 'Love Power' and 'Alfred E. Newman for President'. She keeps taking everything out, laying the stuff on her lap, fingering it like she's counting gold before carefully putting each thing back again. The bus only has to make one sharp turn and she's crawling on the floor, picking up buttons and pictures, but she keeps taking everything out, putting it back again, all the time telling me in a low naggy voice everything she knows about Mick Jagger.

She reminds me of the girl who used to sit on the ground outside the candystore with a pocketbook full of candy bars. When I came out with my Tootsie Roll, she'd show me them and then say 'and I even have a dollar left for more'. I never saw her eating the candy bars. I figured she just kept buying them to show off with. I must have been jealous because once when I got my allowance I spent it all on candy and with my arms full of jelly babies, Milky Ways, jujubes, I stood before her. She didn't say anything, just brought out her own collection. I saw that she had more than I could ever have, that her Hershey bars had melted, her Tootsie Rolls were bent from having lain in her bag for weeks. I sat down on a bench and ate all my candy, chewing without tasting, throwing the wrappers on the ground. I had candy sickness and could not eat my dinner.

By the end of the week we have a few more kids, a black boy with the kind of light skin where you know he must be mixed. He's very smooth and gets in with the back seat crowd without even trying.

I begin sitting with Gloria because I get tired of the other girls complaining about how cliquish everyone is. The chubby boys launch attacks on the back of the bus, diving into the girls who sit on the edges of the seats combing their long hair. 'Cut it out,' they scream and fall into the laps of the jokers just waiting to be used.

Gloria pays no attention to these shenanigans which get so bad that the bus driver, a bald, wide guy named Moe stops the bus and comes rushing down the aisle after them. Maybe he heard them calling him 'Moe the shmo' because he threatens to kick them off the bus. The boys quieted down but after five minutes they're back trying to barge their way in. 'The kingdom,' Gloria calls the crowd at the back, 'You have to be born into it.'

I come home tired in the evenings, the long bus rides, the sun, the hours listening to Gloria take everything out of me. But it's too hot to sleep. I keep searching for a piece of cool sheet, around and around in my bed till the chill air of the early morning washes over me, but then I have to be up to catch the thirteen bus. Something is nagging at me all the time so when I fall asleep I wake up again fast like I'm tumbling in the dark.

18

Sonia

The children sit back against the high metal fence, the girls crouching to protect their bare legs from the burning concrete, the boys tapping out the rhythm with the points of their little flags, their mouths open like thirsty birds as they sing the new song for the fourth time. We have waited all afternoon for the flag day procession. I led my children out to the yard after lunch and we practiced marching two by two behind Richard and Paul who hold our class flag.

The children were told to wear as much white as possible so that the colors of their country would show up against their clothes. Now the red, white and blue crêpe paper sashes across their chests have begun to melt in the sun, the dye staining their white shirts and dresses. All over the yard teachers try to pull the sashes off, but the melting paper sticks to their clothes and the children are left to peel off the bits from their chests.

The mothers will be angry, will blame us, always the teachers. We were nagged for weeks about the day, had to sing patriotic songs to our classes, tell them once again about Betsy Ross, teach them how to handle the flag: how it must be held upright and never allowed to touch the ground.

'Treat it with respect and love as if it were your own mother and father.'

They know it is more valuable than their little lives, for every flag no matter how small holds within its stars and stripes the soul of the country.

'Pick it up,' Linda screeches for the monitors allowed the class flag to topple.

'Kiss it,' Pauline says as a Charley Donnell, the smallest boy in the class, retrieves the flag. 'You've got to kiss it if it touches the ground.'

I do not know where they learned this for to kiss the flag must surely be a desecration. Or does it bring good luck, like kissing the Torah?

I run with the other children trying to reach the scrolls clothed in velvet and damask. Three times the old men march with the Torahs around the edges of the seats and down the center aisle. We push against each other, touching our fingers to our lips, trying to kiss as many Torahs as we can before they are returned to their home at the back of the little stage where the cantor has not stopped singing. My father holds one in his arms. He does not greet me as I kiss my fingers and touch the purple velvet folds, the golden Hebrew letters. He is smiling but not at me, his eyes upraised, his hoarse voice joining the song of adoration which sends us round and around the shul.

Who are we marching for? The mothers haven't been invited. The only people watching are the principal and vice-principal and the mothers and babies in the adjacent playground. And why do we wait and wait? The whole school is out here. Somebody said the music class was still practicing, but their discordant sounds stopped, their instruments abandoned on the hot concrete while they huddle in the shade.

Christine is dressed with care by her mother in a flared white skirt and blouse with a wide collar and bow, two butterfly clips in her frizzy hair. She was smiling all the time the class marched and sang in our corner of the yard, her bony knees raised high like a soldier. Her partner, Suzy Newman, a bug-eyed girl even smaller than Christine with short high pigtails like horns, refused at first to hold her hand. But Christine didn't seem to care.

Nobody touches her anymore. The bigger girls, who like to think of themselves as teacher's helpers, always asking for jobs to do for me like handing out the colored paper and wiping the top of my desk, decided to feel sorry for the girl. They scolded anyone who said a word against her, even though they themselves had joined in the persecution months ago. Christine was their little sister, their puppy, their ragdoll. But the arms they place around her feel no different from the punishing hands she's endured this year. Do they not wonder what is she laughing at when they hadn't said anything funny?

'We're starting,' Mrs. Jacobson announces through her bull horn. The music class begins to group themselves behind her, juggling their hot instruments from hand to hand. The color guard comes forward, two boys and a girl from the smart class of the sixth grade holding the large faded flag which is brought across the school auditorium stage every week in assembly. As the band starts up, they begin marching around the yard, each class joining them until the whole school is marching, their chests stained red and blue in the unwinking sun.

Three times we circle the yard. When the music stops, Betsy Ross, a third grader in a white bonnet with an apron over her white skirt and blouse walks to the center of the yard with a flag draped across her arms. As she waits for George Washington, her face grows red from the strain of holding up her arms. The solemnity is broken by giggles as a boy comes forward wearing pants which stop just below his knees, a white wig, the white powder on his face streaked with perspiration.

Betsy Ross curtseys to him and whispers, 'I have sewn the flag that you requested sir.'

'One star for every state in eternal union?' he asks.

'Yes sir.' She holds out the stiff material.

He turns from her and seems to address some audience in the ground: 'We'll hold the flag high above the battles for freedom and liberty.' Then he places his hand on his heart and everyone says the Pledge of Allegiance with him. The color guard comes forward with the principal who leads them in 'The Star Spangled Banner', 'The Battle Hymn of the Republic' and the new song.

The children are gripped by the song perhaps because they have had to memorize it in such a short time. And it is new, not mouthed year after year in assembly. Their faces turn eagerly towards the principal in her navy blue suit as they sing: 'High snowy mountains, Fields ripe with grain, Homes in the valley. Flocks on the plain. We're blessed with freedom, and never a fear. America, Oh America. Home to our fathers, year after year.'

They march once more around the yard, then leave through the back gate, each class dissolving into children running away from the hot yard.

Irene is waiting for me outside the gate. Her children were among the first to escape, leaving her holding the flag. She has on one of her faces.

'Wasn't that terrible?' I hope that by commiserating I can lift Irene out of her mood. 'Why did they have to make us wait so long? And the heat.'

Irene says nothing to this. She will be difficult and I sigh, as much from the thought of the evening to come as the spent afternoon. 'Thank God it's over.'

'It's not over,' Irene whispers, her hands crushing the folds of the flag. 'I got called in today.'

'What do you mean?'

'She kept asking me was I still a member. It was as if she couldn't believe anyone like me could be trusted to tell the truth.'

'But she has nothing on you. You quit the party a long time ago.'

'Don't be so naive Sonia.'

I start to speak. I want to say I am tired of her calling me naive.

'It doesn't matter when you quit or even if you never joined. You see? It's like I'm infectious.'

'I don't believe it's that bad. All that business with McCarthy is over isn't it?' But I am vague about what has been happening; I shut the television off when the trials came on. 'He's been made a fool.'

'So why are they bothering with me? If it's over why don't they just leave me alone? Can you answer me that?'

'It's only one woman. You talk like there's a whole group interrogating you.'

'Maybe there is.'

'Oh come on Irene. You always take such a negative view of everything.'

'You can talk.'

Why does she take it out on me? As if I don't have problems. I don't have to stay, to stand by the fence in the wasted heat of the afternoon. 'Flat leaver,' the kids called the one who had enough of fighting.

'Just my luck,' Irene says. 'I should've married Harvey.'

The school has dispersed and the yard is empty of all but the principal, the vice principal and a few teachers who begin picking up bits of crepe paper and small cardboard flags which fell from the children's hands as they fled.

Irene looks at the small group through the fence. 'I said to her "my job's okay, isn't it?" She said she thought so. She said by the way they wanted me to teach the 'three' class next year. The "three" class. Can you believe that?'

'So what?'

'Don't you know anything?'

'What are you shouting at me for?'

'Don't you know they're the dummies?'

'Someone's got to teach them.'

'But not me.' Irene presses her finger into her chest. 'Not me. I told her. I got upset. I said "But I've always taught the 'one' class". Always I get the brainy ones. I'm the only one in the school who can challenge them. I said to her "The 'one' class is my class. Everyone knows that". She was so cold to me like I was a criminal.'

'Did she give you a reason why?'

'She said "We've all got to take turns". But you know that's not it. I've been teaching that class for seven years. I've given myself to that class.'

'I didn't know you cared so much. You act like it's just a job. You could be teaching any class.'

'Of course I care.'

'But you were always so scornful of the kids.'

'You never understand do you? You never understand anything beyond yourself.'

'Leave me out of this, will you.' I start to leave but Irene grasps my arm.

'She wanted me to quit. She was hoping I know and maybe I will. Maybe I should.' She lets go of my arm. 'You can leave if you want to.'

She lets the flag drop and presses herself against the fence. 'Who do you think you are? Just who do you think you are? You think you're God?'

'Shush Irene. They'll hear.'

'I hate you,' she whispers to the group in the center of the yard who stand with their backs to her.

Cries come out of her, Irene who never breaks down. Dry sobs, her throat swollen with sorrow. 'I feel dirty. You know what I mean? Like they've got their paws all over me.'

I pick up the flag and put my hand on her back, her dark blue suit consuming all the heat of the day.

'Come on. Let's bring this in and go home.'   But Irene will not leave the fence. I touch her red hair grown pale in the sun. 'You're so hot.'

'I'm burning up.'

19

Helen

It's like playing goldfish. In the beginning the right card can be anywhere. Then you begin to remember which cards you turned over, you make a picture in your mind, you follow the eyes of your friend when you've uncovered one card and are looking for the match. I made a list in my head of all the places the photographs could be in my parents' room. 'Be systematic,' my father's always saying. Whenever I'm alone in the house I make myself look in one of those places instead of always going back to the sweater drawer, hoping she'll put them back, she'll relent.

I begin to know all the smells of the room: the stink of my father's birdseed cologne, my mother's talcum powder, the warm soot on the window sill, the cracked wooden drawers where my mother keeps the clothes she never wears. For I do not recognize the red flowered scarves, the creamy blouses with round collars and bows, the wide belts of soft leather, the shiny black slips which reach almost to the floor on me. 'They hang on you,' she would say. I stand on the bed and look at myself in the wide curved mirror. I'm a scarecrow in her clothes, flapping my arms at my reflection, dancing on their creaking bed.

I enter the walk-in closet they share. When I was little, my mother had to pull me out from the tangle of suits and dresses, the trees of my forest; for the closet led me beyond their bedroom to a cool dark wood. The path wound through my head like a nursery rhyme and I was always pushing against their clothes to get through. There was a sound in the closet my mother could not hear, the breathing of animals waiting for me to turn my back on the shoe-trees climbing up the door.

Now when I flash on the light I see the scratched dull wall beyond the second rail of clothes. Beyond that is my room. My father's hats sit on one long shelf which extends from the front to the back of the closet. On the floor the vacuum cleaner and the suitcases, their satin pockets filled with bathing caps, Band-Aids, mosquito spray. Every summer my father brings out the suitcases, lays them open on the bed and shouts at me to bring in my clothes. But they are empty now; I open each one with a tiny key and let the smell of summer escape.

I sit on the floor of the closet, my head and shoulders touched by my mother's dresses, my father's suits. There can be no other place for the photos. She has thrown them into the flames of incinerator, shaken them out the window into a tree where they float like dead leaves to the ground for some stranger to pick up and wonder about. Who are these people, this black man and white woman under the tree, and why did they care so little?

Then I notice it under a pile of my old games, right in the corner, a Macy's box its sides sealed with scotch tape. First I think it's junk again: playbills, a menu, school notebooks with black and white spotted covers. I almost dump the whole box out on the bed, but remember just in time that my mother might have a special order to things, so slowly I pile one on top of the other in the order I find them: the notebooks, a photo of my grandfather standing with one hand clutching his arm, his union card, little grey books of poetry by someone called Caleb Pink.

It's just a lucky accident they fall out of the first notebook I open. Easy. The photos are in my hands again. But I don't feel anything. I held them in my mind for so long that the actual figures look dull to me, a chubby woman and a tired old black man, as old as my father.

Each page is dated even if it only has a few lines. I can tell it's her from the handwriting even though the notebooks have no name and none of the poems are signed. 'The rain slides down the bus windows, Like tears on an old woman's face.' I blush as I read: 'I lie in my clean white bed. Lovers climb through my body, so cool and perfect. I am so perfect. And they whisper to me of nights.' I turn the pages fast because on each one is an embarrassment; my mother throwing off her clothes, dancing before me naked, laughing in my face for I have never seen her with nothing on.

Then there are pages and pages with the same poem written over and over again, with lines crossed out and added, the whole last part of the notebook full of this crazy poem which I don't understand. Even on the last page she's still changing it. First she calls it 'The Warrior', then 'Stone Shadows' but in the end settles for 'The Earthly Sort' and even dedicates it, as if anyone cared, to Caleb Pink.

THE EARTHLY SORT

The Complaint

Not that I scorn mortal man, only
how to explain, that his is a spasm
a moment before he turns his mouth,
the flesh become word
to shape considerations.

Nightfall, The Museum

The tomb of some clay gone queen
must hold me
till the guards fasten the doors against still creatures
stones cut with the unfathomable.
I emerge
my skin cool glass, nipples like pebbles
my legs have lost their feeling.

He not prominent
not the Pharaoh marching one foot forward in place
or the Greek alabaster stride.
date vague, his maker unknown
cast in obscurity beyond reach of the moon
rude city light
my hands must be eyes.

The chest a black petal, perfection but
for a chipped eyelid, the excavator struggling
to possess, the earth resisting, his hands, the blade slips
Look of readiness, spear grasped as if he hears crowds
stamping through the city
smells wolves descending.

He seems, yes is warm
from summer penetrating even these walls
or from the hands of the furtive
while the guard dreamed, Coney Island rising behind shut eyes.
I touch the thighs, smooth like a young boy's
We lie down together,
still he holds his spear
as if it had become part of him
so we love
awkwardly
struggling for dominion amid stone shadows.

Before morning
before the lone watchman paces the room
I return him to his pedestal
no god has intervened on my behalf
His seed cannot bring forth children of the earthly sort.

I keep closing the notebook, then opening it again to the dirty parts of the poem. It gets easier to read. I no longer have to look at it out of the corners of my eyes. But when I think of my mother, her face keeps changing like the crystal ball in the *Wizard of Oz*. Suddenly I see the laughing black face of the wicked witch in the ruby glass and I'm screaming, my mother next to me saying, 'stop it will you, it's only a picture, it's not for real.'

※ ※ ※

We're riding the waves at Jones Beach when it happens. You have to be careful they don't break over you. I was thrown down once and I flew through a man's legs before I hit the air again. It's as if someone's angry with you, thundering their revenge, beating you down. You crawl away, water up your nose, head aching, thankful to survive. You think you'll never do it again but you're back in five minutes with everyone else.

It's a game of terror. You watch for the big ones, diving down into the foam if you've been caught at the crest. 'Oh no. It's coming!' someone screams like the man who first sees the monster in the horror film, and then we all turn our backs and make ourselves into fish. In the small waves I'm a ballet dancer lifted so gently by my partner. I always twirl in the water afterwards.

I stray beyond the others for the waves seem small today and all the time receding from us as we wait in the flat grey waters, splashing each other and dunking down to keep the shivers away. I keep walking till I meet the wave, the undertow pulling at me like an old friend. I'm not afraid when I see the heads of the others beyond my reach. I'll have the wave first before they can tame it with their screams, before it rushes into the sand and carries back with it the pee of little children. If I keep going I'll land on the down side of the horizon.

When I turn around again I see two heads moving towards me, strange men come to bother me out by myself in the ocean. I try to swim away from them, but they move fast, the life guards come to get me, the two of them holding a little raft between them, telling me to hold on.

'I'm all right,' I shout above the roaring of the sea. I don't want to go in, not with them. But they don't answer. They push the raft under me. I hold on while they swim back with me to the shore. Someone says later they would have knocked me out if I resisted.

Gloria is there with the kids watching when I stumble out of the water. I try to act cool like there could be no possibility I was drowning, shrugging my shoulders and explaining even before I reach them and they can hear what I'm saying that I didn't need to be saved.

'You worried me,' Gloria says, tapping my shoulder with her nail. 'I ran all the way out here because they said you were out too far.'

It's the first time I see Gloria in the ocean. As we walk back she shivers from the brief touch of water on her legs. There's a commotion by her beach chair, girls scattering when they see us approaching.

'I told them to watch my things,' she says.

I hear them giggling into their blankets as they flop down. Gloria's bag lies on its side in the beach chair she always takes with her. She picks up her turquoise terry cloth robe which fell down from the back of the chair as they fled and spends a long time shaking the sand from it. Maybe she doesn't notice the white case on the chair and next to it the little white cap like a doll's yarmulkah which they filled with sand.

The girls are still laughing as she picks it up, tosses the sand back on the beach and begins to wipe the rim with tissues before putting it back in the case. Then she dumps everything out of her bag, each thing, her lipstick, her compact, her bottles of suntan lotion, her glass case, even her keys, she wipes with tissues. When she's through and everything's back in her bag, she turns to the girls, their bodies still trembling with laughter, their faces buried in the blankets.

'You're cowards, do you know that? Filthy cowards.' Then she lies back down on the beach chair, begins to rub those parts of her legs which got wet with suntan lotion.

On the bus the girls are saying that the cap is something you stick up yourself to keep from getting pregnant. I pass by Gloria and sit near the back so I can listen to them. I feel bad but I figure she doesn't want any of us near her, not even me. She is like a sick person.

Gloria doesn't turn up the next day. We wait around the bus till a man from the camp comes by to tell us she quit on them and we wouldn't be going anywhere that week till they find someone else.

'You kids give her trouble?' He looks at the boys.

I know then I won't be going back there for a second month. I tell my parents it's so bad even the counselor quit. I hang around

Orchard Beach with Sheila, walk up and down the hill at Fordham Road letting her talk about Eddie. He came back and then went away again and she is still hung up. 'Such slavery,' she says rolling her eyes. When she gets going she stops in front of me, her eyes searching my face to make sure I am with her, then talks till she gets it all out of her system until the next time. She can be sure I'll hold everything she says to me safe inside; even if she forgets I'll remember, I'll store her secrets like water for the dry times.

20

Sonia

'I wouldn't be caught dead in one of those places.' I speak loud enough for the man behind the deli counter to look up with a grin.

'You don't look dead to me.' He winks and flips over a potato knish.

Why did I order it? Like a stone. A heavy brown pillow, its case hard with grease, will sit in my stomach for hours.

'Just this once.' Irene never pleaded like this. She holds her plate with both hands like an offering.

'Yeah, why not,' the man says with a grin for me.

But he'll not get a smile out of me, the wisecracker. I want to say 'why don't you mind your own business' but then I will look the fool.

'You don't even know what we're talking about.'

'I don't have to, do I?'

I blush. I turn to face Irene. I keep my voice low so he cannot hear, but he has gone back to slicing roast beef. 'But you used to call them marriage markets.'

'So what if they are?' Irene looks annoyed. 'Never mind. I'll go by myself. I'll share a room with God knows who.' She walks to the last row of tables by the wall, sits down with her back to me.

'One knish,' the man shouts though I'm standing right there.

'Imbecile,' I mutter. I lift the plate with the knife and fork resting on the knish off the counter, begin walking towards the table. But I move too quickly; the fork falls and I have to go back and ask for another.

He shakes his finger at me. 'That's what you get.'

'He's obnoxious,' I say when I reach Irene.

'He's just kidding you. Don't be so touchy.'

I say nothing to this. I am always the touchy one. Irene is sensitive.

'So you won't even try once.'

'I don't understand you.'

'Listen I'm not seeing anyone. I figure maybe, maybe I'll meet someone up there.'

'A weekend with a lot of *alter kockers*.'

'So we'll have a good laugh. They can't all be terrible. I had a friend who met a social worker at Grossinger's.' She looks at me. 'Caleb's not calling you. What do you have to lose?'

'Caleb's busy,' I mumble. Maybe we should have time apart to think he said, and I was too afraid to ask him what he meant. Now it has been two weekends but I will not call him.

I lie in my white bed listening to the sounds from the other side of the wall till they become words, the crew cut man moaning to his enormous wife about the heat. Beyond the door the hallway sucks in the night air I spurn and turns it sour. Mom always said that moving made you hotter; if you remain still you might just keep the heat from getting inside you.

'So it comes to the same thing. You're free,' Irene says, 'I just want to get outta here for a few days. For all I know I might not have a job next year.'

'C'mon they're not going to fire you.'

'What if I refuse to take the dummies?'

'You won't. You know you won't. You'll stay on till they give you back your class.'

'It's as if I'm infected. Nobody at school wants to come near me.'

'But nobody knows.'

'You're out of it Sonia. Everyone knows. They know I'm not getting the "one" class. They know why.' She is quiet.

I think how fragile she is, a child in her mother's good suit.

'Don't look at me that way. I don't need your pity.'

'So what do you want from me?' I can never win with Irene.

'I want to go to the mountains.'

'So we'll go.'

'But we've got to really decide. They get busy. If we want to go beginning of August I have to make a reservation now. What do you think?'

'Well maybe.'

'With you that means yes.'

In the darkness outside the hotel I do not see the edge of the grassy hill, the great black gap which is the valley below. He holds me back just in time.

'I think I have night blindness,' I say.

He continues to hold my shoulder, but he's turning his head all the time to look at the lighted building where the band has begun playing again.

'Shouldn't we go back?' he asks.

I suggested we walk from the room where we stood on the sidelines trying to make our words heard over the voices intoning 'one two, cha cha cha'. He said he didn't know these new dances, and I could tell by the way he bent his head towards me, waiting for my words that he was afraid I might want to pull him out on the dance floor. I would have told him not to worry, I cannot dance either, but the worry is his cloak.

The pouches around his mouth contain all the words he cannot speak. Seth is the quietest man I have ever met. Not even Caleb in his moods can speak such silence, such emptiness in which I move like a swimmer in thin blue air. I am sure he is not much older than me, yet his stubbly hair has gone grey and his hands are always picking at the white tufts on his neck his razor has missed. He's as gangly as a teenager, tall and thin with long arms which he keeps folding and unfolding, his bony shoulders in a permanent stoop. I take up all the space when I stand with him.

When we return to the dance, the couples are waltzing. Women drag men onto the floor, laughing at such old fashioned music, some of them trotting through 'The Blue Danube', for they do not know the 'one two three' which the others mouth as they move. As the couples whirl past us, I pull Seth closer to the wall for I fear they might carry us into their merry-go-round.

After the waltz the band plays 'Satin Doll'. The exhausted couples lean on each other, some of the women with their heads on their partners' shoulders as they slow dance around the room. Seth whispers that maybe we can join this one. First he holds me at arm's length and does not stray from the corner where we watched the others. His hand grows more easy on my back, presses me to move into him, to lean my cheek on his shoulder. I am dizzy beneath the swaying lights, the draggy tune the band will not stop playing, as if the floor itself is moving beneath me, me in this strange man's arms drawn closer and closer to the center. I can resist no longer, lean my face against him with my eyes shut.

'You all right?' he whispers.

I press my face harder against his shoulder, my eyes wetting his suit. If he asks me again I will scream and even now sounds come from me muffled by his shoulder, my mouth against the smooth linen.

'Do you want to stop?'

I shake my head. Does he know he smells just like a colored man, even his cologne cannot disguise Caleb.

'You've had a success.' Irene tries to push down the lid of her suitcase. 'If they take your phone number you've had a success. That's what everyone's holding their breath for the last day. Didn't you notice all the girls making themselves available?' She sits down on the edge of her suitcase and snaps it shut.

'You'll ruin it that way,' I say.

'What do I care.' The man who attended Irene all weekend, a doctor from Westchester, has just driven away. I saw her pause after he kissed her, her hand still on his shoulder. The moment had come for him to pull out a piece of paper and pencil, but he turned away, his hands fishing for car keys. She climbed back up the hill to the other women waiting like army brides in the porch of the hotel, their faces questioning her, but she would not say.

'What will Caleb do? The guy couldn't take his eyes off of you all weekend.'

'I won't tell him. He doesn't have to know.'

'They always know. Like dogs they can sniff when another one's been around.'

'You're making a big deal out of nothing. I probably won't even see him again. He's not really my type.'

'He's good looking, so what if he's boring.'

'He's not boring, just quiet. Anyway how would you know?'

'I sat next to him at the cabaret and he had nothing to say for himself.'

'So he's not a blabbermouth.'

'Aha! A sign. You're defending him. You're obviously interested. You never defended Caleb.'

'I didn't need to.'

'Sure. He's full of himself. I don't know how you stood him.'

'You don't know him.' Caleb turning away from me, his broad naked back, his head bent over his writing afraid I will steal from him, for hadn't he seen his words in the poetry I showed him, hadn't he put his finger on whole lines and said I had taken him in? Then he carried me to the bed, me who had been so big my father had ceased taking me on his shoulders when I was still a small child; he drank from between my legs till I gave up my poison.

'You're blushing,' Irene declares, 'which means you're still in love with him.'

There is time. What happened all these weeks could be undone if only I can see him before the numbness takes me over again, my hands paralyzed, my lips too dry to move.

I wait for Irene to disappear behind her curtain before calling Caleb. He is casual in the face of my panic. I will have to wait till next weekend to see him and even then he had only one night to give me.

When I ask why he cannot see me sooner, he is silent then says he is busy, don't I understand how busy he is?

'But it will be too late,' I think.

In the horror movie the lovers flee from a town possessed. Please let me rest she says we have been running for so long I promise I will not even shut my eyes. But she sleeps. What does she dream in that moment for it is only for a moment she forgets him, but this is all the body snatchers need. She wakes with eyes which hold no love for him.

I do not unpack that night. I leave my suitcase standing beside the bed, shut the light and lie naked in the heat without even a sheet to cover myself. Caleb once said only animals and madmen

141

sleep without something to cover them. Through the narrow opening I allow myself for air, I hear Irene opening and closing the drawers to her bureau, the tinny sounds of metal hangers being pushed to one side as she puts back the dresses which served her so ill.

Then I am dropping into the heat, my ears clogged from the descent. My room is being dragged through the streets, my arms so heavy I cannot lift them to knock against the boards above me to tell someone to let me out. Voices come and go in a roar and a crest of silence as if someone holds shells to my ears. I cry out, but though my lips open and my throat vibrates, no sound comes from me.

'Papa,' I scream for I see through the boards the sunlight and the watery grave.

❋ ❋ ❋

Seth steps on the wine glass but no one can hear it cracking against the thick beige carpet. The rabbi lifts the broken pieces in the linen napkin carefully for he does not want bits of glass in his toes when he walks barefoot through the house at night. When I drink from the silver goblet, purple Mogen David spills on the carpet. We are the only ones to notice, the rabbi and myself. I see him look at the stain; he hopes we will leave quickly after the ceremony so he can get the wine out of the carpet before it sinks deep into the wool and becomes part of his apartment.

I have been at weddings where the rabbis go on for a half an hour talking about marriage, quoting from the Talmud and telling amusing fables about tolerance in their warm throaty voices. Like grandfathers they are. But he will not speak in a singsong, forgiving us beforehand all the hatred we might bear each other.

Seth chose him. We went to his shul on Passover. His rich congregation twisted and sighed under his gaze, for who could find comfort in the lean young man, his face white and drawn from study, his voice shrill as he spoke out against the assimilators? Our children are leaving he said, his eyes on the college boys and girls in the audience. The Jews kept their God when all else was taken away from them, had died rather than convert. Why can't they resist the soft blandishments of Gentiles, why can't they be as strong as the ancient Jews who killed themselves up on the mountain? The parents nod their heads but they are bloated with pride for their American children.

Why he is so angry with us? I look at the face of the rabbi as he speaks in the harsh guttural tongue I cannot understand. My father had been in awe of the learned man, had extended his good hand without attempting to speak. The rabbi ignored the others who gathered around him before the ceremony, Leo with his jokes, Leah asking him if he knew this one and that, Julius murmuring his thanks. He beckoned to the two of us to come forward with a gesture almost of impatience.

The sunlight from the bay window behind the rabbi is so brilliant that I can barely lift my eyes when I repeat the words he gives us. Everyone stands in semi-circle behind me listening, but I am sinking in the still heat, then swimming up through the silence to hear a bus pause and then shoot forward into the stream. The rabbi is not touched by the sun; his face remains pale, his long, fine hands were cold as he handed me the goblet, in his dark suit he is like the figures my children used to cut from black paper and paste on white. My face flushes from the heat as he talks about how I as wife and someday mother must be the keeper of our God. For me to stray even for one moment is to lose eternity.

As he stares at me I feel he must know I lay with a Gentile, a colored man whose flesh still burns within me. I nod, hoping to soften his gaze. I came laughing into the rabbi's apartment house. Seth pushed me to set the date, he wanted a religious ceremony, the Manhattan rabbi with a reputation. When I mentioned that one of my friends married at City Hall, he looked at me reproachfully as if I were making fun of our marriage even before it had begun.

I kept away from my family during the engagement but almost every night one of them was on the phone: my mother, my brothers, even Leah, as if to make sure I did not run away. Once Julius took Seth and me out to a Chinese restaurant. His daughter played with the revolving table till the dishes began to fall off and Norma told her to stop. But I was the one who lay across the table large and naked and as helpless as a baby while they turned and turned.

Irene said, 'What's the matter with you?'

'I don't know. I'm just sad.'

'Did you really think you could have stayed with Caleb?'

'It's not him.'

'Then why are you crying? It's inevitable, isn't it for all of us?'

I was calm after that, put on the clothes I bought in Orhbach's: the white nylon blouse with the soft bow collar, the Dacron blue suit which would not wrinkle as we rode up to the Adirondacks.

If I turn now the semi-circle will tighten around me. Why hadn't I realized all these weeks as we prepared, that they bound me so, thrust me before this prophet, who tears Caleb from my body till my loins ache till I mouth his name instead of God.

21

Helen

I smell the cereal and keep to my room till I hear them leave the table and settle into their positions in the living room. They start fighting, not my father's usual barking, my mother's silences, but the low sounds of picking at each other, pick, pick, pick, like chickens.

'Why don't you ever want to try something different?' my mother says.

'But who ever heard of the place? Why can't we go back to The Goldbergs. We were happy there.'

'You were.'

'What was wrong with it anyway? Tell me one thing that was wrong with it.'

'Please, let's not start this again.'

'No tell me. I want to know.'

But she waves him away. 'This sounds cozy.' A strange word for my mother to use. She has the *New York Times Magazine* open on her lap to the small ads on the back.

'But I never even heard of the place.'

'You said that already. They've got a recommendation from the Progressive League.'

'I never heard of them either.'

'Listen to me. It sounds nice. "Comfortable log cabins, home cooking, camp fires every week, a lake with canoeing".'

'But do they have a golf course?'

She ignores his question and reads on. 'Hiking, nature walks, folk-singing and poetry nights, discussion groups, meditation and yoga.'

'But I wanna go on a vacation,' he whines.

I would've taken his side but then he turns on me. 'Your cereal's cold.'

'I don't want any.' Every day the same thing since I quit the camp, the grey mush in a large yellow fiesta soup bowl we never use. He eats his with mounds of sour cream, his head bent over his plate like a horse. My mother pours sugar all over hers so she can't taste it, but I wait till he leaves for work before throwing the whole mess down the toilet. It takes all day to flush it down and bits are still in the bowl when my father returns in the evening. I hear him ask my mother if I've been sick but she never tells on me.

'You'll sit there till you finish it,' he warns just like in the old days but he can do nothing to me now.

Somehow after nagging me he's lost the battle with my mother for she begins tearing out the advertisement. She's drawn into herself, her face has that 'button up your lips and throw the key away' look. No matter how much you yell at her you will not get her even to notice you.

We both watch her for a moment, my father's hands massaging the arms of the easy chair.

'Hey I haven't even read that yet,' my father says.

But she continues tearing, and when she finishes tosses the magazine into his lap and walks out of the living room down the hall to their bedroom.

Geronimo Lodge is not like any place we've ever been before. You have to walk through a little forest to reach your cabin which is made out of logs like they said, but inside rough white walls, a bunk for me, a low wide cot for my parents and a large heavy walnut bureau for our clothes.

'Smell,' my mother says as she stands in the middle of the room with her eyes closed. We take deep breaths of the place, my father with a look of suspicion on his face.

'So?' he says.

'The woods. You can smell them even in here.' She seems to expand as she breathes, her blue A line dress billowing in the drafts my father sends through the room when he opens and shuts the closet and the bathroom doors.

I taste warm earth like spring in the Bronx, the air through the soot like the inside of a leaf. When I was little I used to run faster in the spring gulping the air, but now it makes me thirsty and I cry in the evenings when the smell comes up from the street through the blackened screens.

My father returns to the room. 'No TV,' he declares with a bitter look at my mother.

You have to watch a big old black and white screen with everyone else up at the lodge where on the first night we sit before an open fire listening to one of the waiters play guitar and sing old songs: 'Universal Soldier' and 'Blowing in the Wind'. He lets us know that during the year he plays at some coffeehouse in the Village. Everyone says he's just like Bob Dylan before he got electric. I agree with my father that he sounds like he has a bellyache, but I get the chills when he makes all of us join in on 'This Land is My Land'.

We eat in the lodge at long tables where you have to pass everything. The waiters and chambermaids are all hippies, the girls with everything dangling, earrings, long frizzed-up hair, their breasts unstrapped beneath see-through blouses.

'Letting it all hang out,' my father says with a sneer.

The waiters wear cowboy scarves and leather bands around their heads to keep their hair back. When they can keep still and stop dancing around with their trays, teasing the married women so they'll get a big tip, I read the buttons on their tee shirts: 'End the bombing', 'Anarchy Forever' and 'Penises Unite'. My father made a big stink about that one till the waiter was persuaded by the owner to take it off. Now whenever he sees my father, he pretends to be zippering up his fly. One of the waiters always wears an old jacket with tails over his tee shirt; when he bends over me I smell mothballs and incense and from somewhere inside him an old derelict.

If it wasn't for the lake my father would have made us leave even though we paid for the first week. It's a walk down the hill from the lodge across a field, then through a narrow rock path in the woods. The lake curves out like a quarter moon from the little beach with wooden chairs and a long bench where everyone leaves their towels and where Bernie, the lifeguard, tends the canoes and rowboats and

147

keeps the kids within the roped shallows. He's a short, dark, compact guy with hair so thick on his chest, back and arms that it looks from a distance like he's wearing a sweater. He has a fat gold ring with a black stone on his pinkie and sometimes you can see a Jewish star peeking out of the black nest on his chest.

'He's got a good head on his shoulders,' my father's always saying about Bernie. He's studying for his MBA at Boston University and always has some textbook on accounting or management on his lap. When one of the kids starts horsing around, he throws down the book, pulls a whistle from the black nest and walks slowly towards the lake blowing.

Our cries, his whistle and the low murmurs of grown-ups chatting are the only sounds on the lake whose water is the clearest we've ever known. In the other hotels I'd come up with mud on my chin which was why everyone used the swimming pool. But here you can watch your feet as you walk in, the water soft and chill even on the hot days.

My mother swims slowly but goes deep sinking under the water and then up with a great splash like a sea lion. My father likes to dive from the raft, over and over he swims back, drags himself up, shakes himself free of the lake, then breaks the water again.

I've heard that at night when Bernie lies on his bunk reading his textbooks, scratching his fuzzy chest, the waiters and chambermaids go skinny dipping in the soft waters and lay each other on the raft, on the beach where my father likes to discuss his hardware store.

Sometimes we run into the owner, Mr. Rosenberg, a small old man in Bermuda shorts with white hair which begins at ear level and is somehow scooped over his bald head. Geronimo Lodge has been going since before the war, when he let a few rooms, served kosher food and called it 'Jerusalem in the Catskills'. He kept buying up land and building but it was his son Josh returning from years on a kibbutz who set up the long tables for communal meals, brought in the hippy staff, started advertising in *The Village Voice* and the *New York Times* and renamed it after a defeated Indian chief.

Now he runs the place. Big Josh with a black beard and Afro hair, like a bear making the plates shake as he walks through the dining room or before the fire with a logs in his arms, his hairy thighs so thick he can hardly crouch down. Everyone says he likes to fool around with the chambermaids, every summer a new one, the girls half his age and him with a son nearly in college.

Nobody is from the Bronx here. When my mother tells them where we live, they look surprised or nod their heads slowly like they're trying to remember. 'We used to live there but we moved when Bonnie was three to Long Island.' Nate who's a professor at NYU says the Bronx isn't really the city. But how can they know my mother says, they haven't taken the subway north in years.

These people. The women are all busy, not like my mother mooning about. They talk about their classes at the New School, their jobs as social workers and teachers. 'Why haven't you gone back?' one of them asks my mother. She shrugs, says she's had it up to here with teaching, points to me and says she has enough on her plate.

'This is where old lefties come to die,' my mother's old friend says. Mrs. Slaven arrived the second week we were there with her eight year old daughter Phoebe who is too shy even to ask anyone to pass her the bread. Children eat with adults here, no separate teen table; we're supposed to be one big happy family. Mrs. Slaven gives me the once over then turns to my mother with a sarcastic expression: 'You sure she's your daughter?'

They haven't seen each other for fifteen years. My mother's old roommate Irene. She looks like an elf with her short brittle red hair, too bright to be real, her sharp face, her mouth full of acid my father says. She tells my mother right away about how she divorced her husband: 'My shrink said why don't you do something for yourself?'

My mother can't take her eyes off her all through dinner: 'Imagine meeting you here. Just imagine.' But Irene acts like they've never lost touch, jabbering about her problems while my mother listens.

'Eat up,' Irene says to Phoebe whose sad freckle face is always looking for some safe haven. 'You dawdle over your food.'

'She's cute,' my mother says.

'She's her father's daughter,' Irene says. 'When I look at her I see why I stayed with him for so long.' She brushes Phoebe's hair from her face, but there is no need for it is short, a pixie cut like her mother's and not getting into her food like mine. I'm always picking bits of dried ketchup from the ends.

My father nags at me to cut it short: 'I can't see your face,' he says and sometimes when he passes me in the hall, he pulls my hair back with his fingers: 'Get it off your face why don't you? That's why you have pimples.' He just doesn't like me looking like a hippy.

With all this attention Phoebe stops eating. Her mother has her arm around her now and she stares at my mother and me, her shyness gone.

They talk all the time in the front yard of the lodge or by the lake. Sometimes I see them strolling down the road, my mother with her arms folded over her sundress, her face mysterious in twilight.

Phoebe never leaves her mother. She hasn't found a friend at the hotel so she runs in front of the two of them as they walk, reaching for her mother's hand when it is not gesticulating. She rocks herself on one of the wide arms of Irene's chair, bathes her Barbie dolls in the lake while they swim.

'I told myself I wouldn't buy her one but I gave in,' Irene says. 'Can you believe it, me buying my daughter one of these plastic women?' She grabs the doll from her daughter. 'Look at the feet.' We look at Barbie; half naked, her blonde hair full of mud, she is forever on tiptoe. 'She's got feet molded to fit high heels. What a message!'

Phoebe reaches for her doll, the only aggressive move I see her make. Irene lifts it high above her then drops it with snort into her daughter's outstretched hands.

'My women's group was very critical but then they're all younger than me, they don't have kids. Your standards get lowered when you have children, don't you think?'

I don't hear my mother's reply for Dean, Josh's son comes by and I want to make sure I'm in the water when he is. It's always like that, I hear a question without an answer or an answer which makes no sense because I haven't heard what went before.

Not like I'm chasing Dean. He spoke to me first. One day down at the lake, he stopped to look at the book I was reading. His slender brown body was shivering from the water but he stayed talking to me, asking me my grade and what high school I would go to. Dean's a senior at Music and Art, three grades ahead of me. He's known for a long time that he's going to be a composer. His voice is soft, somehow he can be quiet even while he is speaking.

'You didn't even like her,' my father is saying. 'You couldn't wait to get away from the apartment. Don't you remember?'

My mother washes the blueberries I picked. The reddish brown tops of her breasts show over her halter top. When she doesn't answer, he grabs his towel, slams the screen door behind him.

Irene has a special voice for my father. 'So how are you this morning Seth?' Her small elf mouth ready to laugh at what he might say. She watches as he piles waffles on his plate, douses them with butter and maple syrup.

'Uh oh, cholesterol.'

'I'm on vacation,' he speaks with his mouth full of waffle, his lips shiny from the syrup, his beady eyes like a wild animal.

Me she never speaks to except to say to my mother that I look like a late developer and isn't my bra letting me down? But she stares, sharp little looks like she's getting her knife and fork into me. Once when I came to them dripping from the lake, my arms outstretched for a towel, I heard her say, 'She won't be like us will she?'

My mother shook her head slowly. 'She won't be like anyone.' Smiling up at me, a real smile not sarcastic as she rubbed my shoulders dry. She's daydreaming all the time now. I have to ask her everything twice. 'What dear?' she says like I'm her little girl again.

'You follow him like a dog,' my father says. But if I'm around when Dean wants to go canoeing and the waiters are setting up, he might ask me to take an oar. Once when I was sitting outside the lodge reading but really waiting for him, he roughed up my hair as he walked by. You have to make yourself available. That's what I read in *Seventeen*. And waiting around is not the same as chasing.

Josh is divorced. Someone said his wife is a Creole, and that Dean might have some black blood from way back, why he is so dark, his chest the color of earth, his fine black hair falling over a forehead too large for the rest of his body. Irene says he's a real Jew. When I ask her what she means she looks secretive, then says, 'He's got liquid eyes.'

But to me they look frightened like the eyes of a deer we caught crossing the road when my father took us to town. I thought at first it was a statue put in the road for vacationers to look at, for it was perfect, its head so still as if fear had turned it to stone.

'Stop!' my mother yelled, 'Will you?'

'Okay, okay. I saw him. I already saw him.' My father rested his arms on the wheel and looked at the deer sideways. 'He should know better.'

'We're the ones who scared him,' my mother whispered.

'What are you whispering for? You think he can hear you at this distance?'

'Shush. We're the ones who don't belong.'

Just then the deer looked away from us, leaped across the road and disappeared into the trees. It was as if it had never happened: my father drove on, my mother lapsed back into silence and we were soon walking around the Teepee Crafts Store in Mountaindale, ice cream sandwiches dripping down our fingers as we looked at cedar jewelry boxes painted with rowboats and pine trees, and Indian peace pipes made in Japan.

Dean likes to hang around with the waiters but his father doesn't want him serving. He has him adding up figures on his calculator in the mornings but Dean's mind is elsewhere and he makes mistakes. I can hear Josh hollering at him from all the way out on the front lawn where I'm sitting with my book, waiting as usual. In front of me women lie on their backs in the grass with their eyes shut, their legs outstretched, their hands open like beggars.

'Let the sounds from outside pass through you,' the yoga teacher drones, 'Let your mind be a sieve.' But everyone is listening as Josh yells 'Can't you do anything right?'

Irene calls Dean a Jewish prince. 'All he ever does is walk around all day half naked displaying himself.'

At night I've seen him get in the car with Felix, one of the waiters. They drink rum cokes at a bar in town which doesn't look at IDs.

Felix is part Argentinean; tall and well built in a bony sort of way, with thick curly black hair and beard. He'd be good looking if it weren't for his bad skin and beaky nose. He always wears just one earring, a dangling one, sometimes a feather or a piece of bone set in silver like a tooth.

Felix is everyone's favorite waiter. He's quick and never makes mistakes. The women like to tease him, even pinch his ass. 'How is it this morning?' they ask him.

He calls me 'Miss Helen' in a false Southern accent and my father 'sir'.

'Madam, can I serve you personally with some French toast?' he asks Phoebe, then looks solemn while she tries to hide her smile. But before my mother's sad, heavy face he does not joke.

We're sitting before the fire playing Trivia when Dean comes in and asks me to go for a walk. I blush because he's asked me in front of my parents and Irene and everyone is watching our backs as we leave together. He walks with his head bent, his arms folded as if he were figuring out something, 'chewing it over,' my father would say. I know he's not thinking about me so I'm surprised when he takes my hand. I don't know why I'm back in fifth grade practicing square dancing with the boys, the teacher saying 'Meet your partner.' We bang heads in the center. 'Now join hands.' The boys squeezing our fingers to show how much they didn't want to dance with us.

We cross the field, Dean holding my hand loosely almost as if he wouldn't mind if I pulled away. On the dark path through the woods he stops, presses his mouth to mine, dry lips to dry lips. My first and it's all over quickly. We walk on. When we reach the lake and can hear the voices of waiters he drops my hand.

'My father's got some new girlfriend,' he says, his voice bitter as he watches the waiters cavort in the lake.

'You mean someone here?'

'No. He goes into the city to see her. They stay in her studio. She's an artist.'

Felix calls out, making motions for us to come in, but Dean shakes his head. We watch them splash each other then flop like great white fish on the raft.

'Did you ever wish you could be born all over again?' Dean asks.

'You mean to different parents?' But you would not be you wishing to be someone else. That was the scary part. If you were born again you became a stranger.

'No what I mean is.' He looks at me for a moment. Maybe what he sees disappoints him for he says, 'Oh forget it.'

I'm getting bitten only I can't complain not like I would to my mother. Can't say I'm bored standing here watching the waiters fool around on the raft.

Felix begins wrestling with a smaller man whose face I can't see, their bodies in slow motion. He's showing off. Why we're so important I can't understand. The two of them do a tango closer and closer to the edge of the raft till his partner falls in and Felix raises his arms in a mock triumph. Then he beckons again but his fingers seem to call only to Dean.

A red moon appears like a huge stop sign above the trees. Dean backs away from the water's edge and begins to walk fast up the path we came, me running behind him.

The next day I'm dancing everywhere remembering the kiss even if it didn't feel like anything. I run up behind my mother and Irene as they cross the field with Phoebe. Irene saying, 'He never remarried you know. Do you ever think what it would have been like if you had stayed with him?'

'But it wasn't like that.'

'Like what?'

'You know. Like you're making it out to be.'

'Don't give me that. You were in love with the guy.'

My mother makes one of her 'leave me alone' gestures but Irene keeps on talking. 'Don't you ever think what if? I'm always thinking what if. My shrink says I torment myself.'

'So don't torment me.'

'But everything's changed now. Now if you met him, well it could work out.'

'Do you really think everything's changed? Because if you do you're more naive than I thought,' my mother says, her voice so full of scorn that I stop myself from putting my hands over her eyes, but she senses me and turns. She stares at me as if trying to figure out what I heard.

'So you condescend to walk with us,' she says finally.

I scamper away into the tall weeds which burn my bare legs. In the heated silence two heads appear, Felix and Dean, their backs to me, their legs stretched out in front of them flattening the long grass, Felix's hand stroking Dean's head.

Their voices sound far away like conversations in a bus station when you doze off. Murmurs. I'm on my hands and knees, crawling so they won't know I've been and seen them. But the grasshoppers jump away from me and I hear Dean say, 'What was that? Was that somebody?'

'Don't worry. It was nobody. Just the wind through the grass.'

I'm running from them across the hill, past my mother and Irene down the wooded path where he stopped to kiss me.

'Hey,' my mother says because I nearly crash into her, but I don't stop till I reach the lake.

'Whoa,' Bernie says, 'no running.' He shakes a finger at me and winks.

Hairy ape. I don't know why I hate him grinning at me like he's the reason.

I pull off my clothes like I'm on fire. He's shouting, 'don't run' at me when I clump down the wooden platform then out to the diving board where I don't even try my new dive. I just hold my nose and jump.

I remember the time coming home from school in a rush because I had to go to the bathroom bad. I went to the wrong floor but didn't realize till the door opened and a strange woman

155

appeared holding the opening of her blouse together, the man on the sofa behind her hiding himself. She had a funny smell. The pee came out of me as I stood there, and she said, 'You'll have to tell your mother to come clean it up.'

'What's the matter with you?' my mother asks because when I come out of the water I lay face down on my towel by her chair without even drying myself.

'Nothing.' I speak with my mouth on the towel. I never told my mother about the pee and the woman with a smell like an animal cage.

Friday before Labor Day weekend and Josh is handing out black masks at breakfast.

'What's this for?' my father asks though he knows.

'Carnival,' Josh says.

It's a tradition at Geronimo. At the end of the summer, before everyone goes home they have a party with prizes for the most outrageous costume.

'You come as you really are,' Felix whispers in my father's ear, then sashays around him picking up dirty plates.

'That won't be hard for you,' my father says. He's pissed off because the cook put whole-wheat flour in the waffles.

'Don't be such a killjoy,' I say even though I'm not feeling too bright myself.

'He's just an old fogey,' Irene pipes up.

This is too much for my father. He leans across the table, eyes bulging, his angry bullfrog look. 'So what are you coming as?'

'To quote my daughter, "that's for me to know and you to find out."'

Usually Josh announces a theme like Greeks and Romans or gangsters and molls but he got so depressed after last year's Fifties night that he decided this carnival would be a free for all.

My father surprises me at the last minute. He winds one of my mother's kerchiefs around his head, sharpens the point of a stick and comes as a pirate. My mother laughs at him but I can see he's enjoying himself, waving his stick around, swooping down on my mother, shouting, 'Now I've got you my proud beauty.'

Irene looks like herself only with a little black hat like a crab she picked up at the Good Will store in town, a dowdy dress and red red lipstick. She carries an iron she borrowed from the lodge and box of Tide. She's a Fifties housewife.

'I'm us,' she tells my mother, 'Like we never were twenty years ago.'

Phoebe is a princess in her mother's dress, a crown cut from a cereal box above her freckle face, lips as bright as Irene's, eyes full of wonder.

I drag around all Saturday thinking I'll stay in the cabin with the insects till my mother says, 'Why don't you come as a beatnik like you did last Halloween. You looked cute.'

One of the chambermaids lends me her beret. I swipe a palette and brush from the arts and crafts room, put on my black tights and my father's shirt. Irene says I look like a whore which pleases me.

My mother doesn't dress up but for some reason she wears the black mask.

The room is warm and dreamy: red lanterns, a strobe light blinking the rainbow, Christmas streamers dangling from the ceiling, the Righteous Brothers singing 'You've lost that loving feeling'. Josh is a sheik serving golden punch he calls elixir. Cleopatra, Groucho Marx and a zebra wave to me as they dance by.

'I wish I had dressed up. I don't know why I didn't,' someone says. Because you don't feel silly once you enter the room. Like jumping in the lake after a heat wave the water so warm and silky you never want to come out. When you do because your mother says your lips have gone purple the cold air is like a slap in the face like you're being born only everyone knows already who you are.

I'm looking for Dean, hoping he'll see my eyes lit up with shadow and pencil. The oldies sigh for Josh has put on Nat King Cole and soon they dominate the dance floor, moving like a slow merry-go-round. Even my mother and father are out there.

When the door opens, we're all too dozy to notice though I feel the draft and think maybe it's Dean. As the number ends a crowd starts to form at the far end of the room everyone clapping and whistling.

First I think Felix is dressed like a woman for I see two black yarn braids, but I get closer, stand on tiptoe to see he's naked to the waist and barefoot with just a little loincloth over his ass. Why does he shock everyone so when his costume is only a headdress of feathers he must have picked up at the Teepee Crafts Store in town, a string of beads and bracelets worn high over his biceps? He hasn't even painted himself. It's the way he's standing, straight and proud, his tanned muscular body as dark as any Indian. He's shaved and with his beak nose, his black shiny eyes, he looks like a hawk, the scars from his acne like war paint.

People are laughing because he's brought a canoe with him, all the way up from the lake he dragged it. Nobody notices Dean dressed like a cowboy, a lasso around his neck.

'Geronimo!' someone shouts.

Felix smiles. 'Am I going to have to dance with one of these palefaces?'

'Isn't he gorgeous?' I hear one of the women say.

'Like a god.'

I think of the Indian on the wall of the Dollar Savings Bank back in the Bronx. In a huge mosaic mural behind the desks where my mother took me to open my first account, he's shaking hands with Jonas Bronk. He's not looking at him but down at us: at the tellers behind their bronze cages, the savers writing on high glass tables, at my mother bending down to show me my bank book: 'Look Helen. Look at your name. Now you're a real person.'

When I was little I used to stand in the middle of the bank while my mother went to the teller and stare up at him. I couldn't understand why everyone was ignoring my Indian. He's enormous and almost naked, the red beads he just received for his land like blood on his hands.

Soon one after the other the women are cutting in. They can't get enough of Felix.

I edge near to Dean hoping like a fool that he'll ask me to dance. He says hello to me in a dull voice, his eyes staring beyond me to Felix.

Josh turns off the lights leaving only the strobe flashing over our faces. Everyone is dancing, their black masks whirling past me as I stumble out the door. It's brighter outside under the porch light of the lodge. My mother's standing alone looking down the hill.

'I wanna go back,' I say.

She doesn't say anything, doesn't even shrug her shoulders like she's heard.

'I said I wanna go back now.'

'So go.' She still standing there with her back to me, her voice all husky like she's been crying, only I know she hasn't. She never cries. 'Your father's still in there. You can go back yourself if you want to.'

She knows I hate walking alone at night down the wooded path to our cabin, that I fear the moment when I turn on the light and surprise the bugs.

I can hear Josh make some announcement inside, then some clapping and laughter. People start coming through the door as if it's all over.

'They must have given out the prizes,' mother says as she turns towards the lodge.

Felix comes out, starts walking down the hill with Dean trailing behind. We watch them stroll across the field, Felix waiting up for Dean before they disappear into the woods. I know they'll be down at the lake, fooling around with each other on the raft and I run forward and let myself fall to the ground. I'm crying into the grass when my mother comes up behind me.

'What is it?' She tries to pull me up.

'Leave me alone.'

'You must get up.'

'No,' I wail and dig my hands deeper into the earth. I'm pulling up grass in handfuls like it's my hair.

'Is it that boy?' But she gets no answer from me.

'Listen to me.' She's crouched behind me still pulling at my shoulders. 'Nobody's so important you should aggravate yourself so.'

How would you know I want to say you never cared for anyone except a black man you keep from everyone even yourself.

'Let go of me.'

'Will you get up then?'

I want to bury myself there, reach into the warm earth so far that I will never hear or see again. I listen to her breathing, short hard breaths because running after me and then crouching is painful for her. She carries so much weight around all the time my father says.

I lift my head. I hear her sigh, then push herself up to standing. I get up too fast and nearly lose my balance I'm so dizzy. She reaches out to steady me, then puts her arm around my shoulders for she knows I cannot stand alone.